Aggie

Edna Forrest

LEUKAEMIA RESEARCH

HODGKIN'S | LYMPHOMA | MYELOMA

First Published 2006

ISBN 0-9543407-5-2
Published by
MM Publishing
Longridge
Sawbridgeworth Road
Hatfield Heath
Bishop's Stortford CM22 7DR

Printed by
rpm print & design
Chichester
West Sussex

Design and Typesetting
by Diane Parker

Cover Design by Monica Clark, Without an E Ltd.

For Jock

My grateful thanks to our daughter Gillian and son-in-law Bill for their valiant and relentless pursuit of my numerous spelling mistakes and punctuation errors.

Thanks also to Diane Parker and Monica Clark. Without an E Ltd.

With love + best wishes
Tanya + Mick
Edna Forrest

LEUKAEMIA RESEARCH

HODGKIN'S | LYMPHOMA | MYELOMA

Chapter One

"Miss Maud won't be joining yer for dinner. 'Er artheritis is playing up somethin' awful to day."

Aggie Brown sniffed as she surveyed the assembled company with baleful eyes. Aggie didn't like visitors. She felt she had enough to do looking after her mistress.

Aggie had started in service with the Hepplewhites fifty seven years previously, when she was thirteen. Her birth during the miner's strike of nineteen twenty-six, had been another unwelcome event in the life of her parents. One baby after another had followed with annual monotony, six surviving, six dying in infancy and so Aggie had been well versed in the art of bringing up children with a meagre income coming in. She could ease a cough with butter, sugar and vinegar. Rid tiny bellies of wind with cinder tea, made by infusing a red-hot coal in water and feeding the residue to a suffering baby. She could make enough Yorkshire pudding to feed all the children, dulling their appetite for the minute portions of meat which followed. As her mother had 'a little cleaning job', Aggie, as the eldest, was the one who had to skip school when any of her brothers and sisters were ill. And she was the one who helped her father to shovel coal into the cellar…coal which was part of his wages and was dropped on to the pavement by a company lorry.

Resentment brewed and festered inside her as she watched her siblings and peers play hop-scotch, kick-can, skipping with discarded lengths of clothes-line and whipping their chalk coloured spinning tops. Her tiny back ached and her skinny arms trembled as she wielded a shovel taller than herself. And resentment against her parents grew as she watched the households who had limited their families to two or three, enabling them to enjoy a few little pleasures in life. Her friends had new dresses, made specially and kept secret, for the Whitsuntide Monday walk, while she had to wear hand-downs given by various cousins. The same friends enjoyed the odd trip to the seaside, returning home with faces smeared with toffee apples and candyfloss, bellies filled with fish and chips and shrimps. They would all sit together on donkey-stoned steps outside Aggie's house, eager to tell her of the wonderful time they'd had and ask why she hadn't come with them.

Aggie breathed a sigh of relief when she walked out of the door of the two-up and two-down miner's cottage for the last time, carrying in her tiny hands a brown paper carrier bag containing a spare pair of navy-blue knickers, vest, liberty bodice, flannelette underskirt and half-a-dozen home-made sanitary towels, 'just in case', although her mother never actually told her what the 'just in case' might be.

With her mother's parting words of 'be'ave thi sen' ringing in her ears, she was about to start work as scullery maid in the establishment of Mr and Mrs George Hepplewhite, gentlemen farmers.

Her departure from home had not been a sad day, but a day of rejoicing for all. One less mouth to feed, three children instead of four sharing a lumpy bed, a little less tugging of scanty bed coverings on a cold frosty night. This made no difference to the two remaining children who, together with the odd mouse, slept on a palliasse laid out on the floor. But they had all benefited from the few extra shillings a week. Aggie's wage, which was paid directly to her mother.

The rejoicing was not limited to Aggie's family. It spread over Aggie like the warmth of hot porridge on a freezing cold morning. There was no room in her chilled heart for any love for her siblings or her parents. She felt not the slightest pang of regret at leaving them. As they waved her goodbye, she stuck out her tongue, cocked a snook...and that was the last she ever saw of them.

....

The arrival of Aggie in 1939...just after the start of World War 2...to... Bishop Grange, home of the Hepplewhite dynasty had passed unnoticed by George Hepplewhite. George spent most of his time away on business, even though he'd avoided being called up into the armed forces by convincing the War Office that he physically worked his farm and was needed on the home front. But to his wife Sarah, who was expecting their first child, soon to be followed by a second, Aggie became indispensable and was quickly elevated to something more than a scullery maid, although her duties were never clearly defined.

For Aggie, the move to Bishop Grange and its unaccustomed life style was one of sheer delight. She'd longed for privacy and as soon as she realized that she'd a room of her own, free from bugs, that she didn't have to help peg a rug in her spare time and that she didn't have to fight for the last slice of bread, she decided that this old, rambling, comfortable country house was where she wanted to spend the rest of her life. The large, impressive entrance hall and wide staircase was flanked by portraits of handsome, be-whiskered Hepplewhites and their full bosomed, bare-shouldered ladies who very soon became, in her eyes, her family.

Sarah Hepplewhite was a hard taskmistress, sometimes driving the servants to the very limit of their endurance with her dictatorial manner, but to the surprise and annoyance of the rest of the staff she developed a soft spot, a genuine affection for Aggie. It was she and not the housekeeper who gently propelled the girl into that hallowed sanctum, the drawing room, after finding her with a home-made sanitary towel dangling from her fingers, her thin body racked with heart-rending sobs, screaming that she was bleeding to death. And it was Sarah who scrubbed the girl's hair with carbolic and with Derbac soap after the rest of the staff had complained she had nits.

Over the years, Aggie had repaid this uncharacteristic kindness from middle-class to working-class with doglike devotion. She'd toiled for no wages when hard times hit the family, Mr Hepplewhite having invested heavily in huge stacks of soap, dubiously acquired via the 'black market', only to find that demand decreased when rationing eased. And she celebrated with them as prosperity returned when the London foreign exchange market re-opened after twelve years of closure, looking after the two children, Maud and Grace until they went to boarding school.

Prior to the occupation by the Germans of the Channel Islands in July 1940, as many families as possible were evacuated from there and Bishop Grange was selected as 'likely to be a suitable billet' for several evacuees from Guernsey. Delivered to the house by kindly Women's Voluntary Service workers, the unfortunate children were soon left in no doubt that they were not welcome and Aggie and her mistress exchanged triumphant and conspiratorial glances as the tearful young victims of war were led away by their dispirited escorts to find other accommodation. Enveloped in its own time warp, no outside influences were going to be allowed to disturb the peace and tranquility of Bishop Grange.

In 1952, whilst the country and the Hepplewhites were mourning the death of King George Vl, George Hepplewhite died from a hunting accident and although Aggie outwardly mourned with the family, she inwardly rejoiced at the master's death, having secretly hated and despised him for years. Aggie had learned to hide her feelings behind an inscrutable mask, although the

3

mask slipped some years later and she cried bitterly and inconsolably when her mistress died tragically as a result of an accident in the home. Neither of the daughters had married and after their mother's death Aggie had stayed on, serving both of them until Miss Grace's untimely death from diphtheria. Aggie also caught the disease but recovered, revealing a remarkable resilience,
considering her early diet of bread and dripping. She continued to look after Miss Maud with the same dogged devotion she'd shown to Sarah, her mother.

At thirteen, Aggie Brown had been a scrawny, unattractive child, with spindly legs and matchstick arms, sparse hair, sallow complexion and tiny pig like eyes that darted swiftly from person to person as if perpetually watching a tennis match. At seventy, Aggie was an older edition of that child. The years had done nothing to enhance her appearance.

Chapter Two

Leo Hepplewhite, aged fifty five, stuck out his tongue at the black-clad, tiny but formidable retreating back of his cousin's faithful servant, then looked around shamefaced at the rest of the gathered guests.

"Leo," whispered Pippa, his young partner, "behave yourself."

Leo laughed humourlessly. "I do apologise for that childish behaviour but…well…returning to this mausoleum brings back memories. Not all happy ones, I may add. I've had many a scuff round the ear from those bony hands, I can tell you."

The party of eight were gathered in the sitting room where they had been waiting for their host to appear. They'd arrived at varying times during the afternoon and as most of them had never met Maud Hepplewhite, Aggie's announcement left them in some disarray, unsure of what to do next. They hadn't been introduced to one another and were finding conversation difficult.

The room, although comfortably furnished with green leather settees and matching armchairs, was oppressive with its deep red flock wallpaper and dark wainscoting. But the cold, dismal late February evening was tempered by a log fire burning fiercely in the large Adam style fireplace, the logs occasionally spitting out their knots vehemently as if objecting to having been placed there. The ancient, oak long-case clock, ensconced in the shadow of a dark corner, chimed mournfully, its ponderous ticking and the hypnotic swing of its brass pendulum informing the intruders that *it* belonged here.

Someone broke wind quietly and a disconcerting silence followed, one of those uncomfortable silences when everyone feels someone should speak, but no-one does.

Pippa giggled and Leo frowned, motioning her to pull down her skirt which was now revealing a pair of shapely legs. She stopped giggling immediately, tugged at the offending skirt and tried to sink deeper into the armchair. A short, middle-aged balding man, dressed in a well pressed dark pinstriped suit and freshly laundered snow-white shirt, coughed dryly, averting his eyes from the girl's dimpled knees. Slowly, he removed his brown tortoiseshell framed spectacles and polished them.

"Perhaps we'd better introduce ourselves."

Leo stood swiftly to his feet. "Well…seeing as I'm family, I'll start. I'm the nephew. Leo Hepplewhite." He paused dramatically and looked around. "Might as well say it. I'm…heir to the throne, figuratively speaking. The last of the Hepplewhites. Well…will be when she…er…when cousin Maud goes. My father was Ernest Hepplewhite, George's young brother. There were just the two of them. My father died shortly after I was born so I never knew him. I'm Maud and Grace's cousin. Well, Grace is dead, of course. Two years younger than Maud, she was. About my age. Diphtheria." He frowned. "Or was it Pneumonia. Probably Pneumonia with this bloody awful Yorkshire climate. Freeze the balls off a brass monkey." A sharp intake of breath from one of the women brought a spurious apology. "Sorry ladies. True though. Wouldn't come back to live in this part of the country, not for a gold pig."

Pippa giggled at his further reference to the animal world. Pippa was an inveterate giggler, a nervous habit she resorted to when she had difficulty expressing herself, not having a prolific command of the English language. "He's always saying that." She blushed as all eyes turned to her. "About a gold pig, I mean," she finished lamely.

Leo glowered at her and she wriggled, making another vain attempt to pull her skirt over her knees.

Returning his gaze to the other guests, he continued. "So, as I'm sure you will agree, I'm an interested party in this carry-on. One of the principal players, I suppose."

The balding man frowned. He was not of the opinion that Leo's kinship gave him precedence over himself in the pecking order of introductions. His family firm of Gough, Gough, Gough and Turpin had been representing the Hepplewhites long before Leo was born and that, in his eyes, gave him seniority in this household over mere kinship.

"This is hardly a 'carry-on' Mr Hepplewhite…Leo. My name is Gough. Harry Gough. Leo and I haven't met before," he explained to his audience, "even though our firm has handled the Hepplewhite's affairs for …well…a long time. That's because, I'm afraid, he has not visited Miss Maud for several years."

He refrained from adding, 'even though he is her only relative', but paused and pursed his lips, indicating that he did not approve of Leo's absenteeism. "Miss Maud is wanting to sell the property which, as you all know, is why we are here. It…will be a sad day for this area. The Hepplewhites have farmed in South Yorkshire for centuries. Provided a lot of employment over the years. So of course… there's great concern over what the property will be used for. There are bound to be objections to any change of use. Our mandate…the reason we have been invited here for the week-end, is to try and thrash out the best solution for everyone concerned." He paused and coughed. "Without publicity."

As if it were an afterthought, he nodded towards a bespectacled lady of ample proportions which were not all, unfortunately, in the correct position, her bosom seemingly having slipped to either side of her body and her buttocks sticking out shelf-like, so much so that it would have been possible to adorn them with knick-knacks. All this was topped with a tiny head, covered in corrugated waves achieved by a tight perm, obviously recently executed, the smell of the perm lotion permeating the air.

"This is my" he cleared his throat noisily, "better half. My wife Mrs Gough. Fran."

The similarity between the names Fran Gough and van Gogh was not lost on the other guests and a few surreptitious smiles passed between them. And Maggie McCriel, architect and a devotee of the arts spent several delicious moments with a cruel, mental image of a Renoir painting of a nude and voluptuous Fran.

Pippa giggled again only to be stopped once more by a dark glare from Leo. She was now losing interest in the proceedings and eyed her partner thoughtfully. She didn't like his eyes. Too small. Too close together. He wasn't bad looking in a rough, peasant sort of way but she thought his drooping, walrus moustache made him look miserable. She thought he should have been more…well…refined looking. After all, he'd been to public school, trained to be an accountant, although he'd failed his exams and now did 'something in the city'. She wasn't sure what he actually did in the city and she didn't really care. He kept her in a manner that she could never have afforded on her own and gave her a generous allowance. They lived in a flat in St. John's Wood, so she assumed whatever it was he did, he did it pretty well.

Pippa was an actress. Well… she'd worked in repertory for a couple of seasons, been on the television once and auditioned for a West End show, albeit unsuccessfully. However, from that audition she'd found work as a hypnotist's assistant and it was there she'd met Leo. The great Marvo had been booked to work a nightclub in Soho. Leo had been with a party of business men who'd persuaded him to volunteer to go on stage. He'd proved to be a perfect subject and was putty in the hands of the Master who had convinced him that he wanted to strip down to his underpants. This action had delighted the inebriated minds of a party of men who were capable, with consummate ease, of manipulating vast sums of money at the touch of a button.

Pippa found 'The Great Marvo' totally obnoxious but he paid her well and she had to admit the man was a genius in hypnosis. He had qualified in medicine, using hypnosis as an aid but had been struck off the medical register when it was discovered that he was also using his hypnotic powers as an aid to satisfy his over active sexual appetite. Pippa was streetwise and had learned at an early age how to fend off any amorous advances with a well directed knee and the pair had developed a mutual respect for one another.

There was a knock on the door and a red faced cook entered the room.

"Dinner's ready. Get yer sens in now."

Harry Gough coughed and replaced his now well polished spectacles. Sighing, he said apologetically, "Perhaps we should go in. I think there is a shortage of staff at the moment. I'll lead the way, shall I?"

He stood and walked across the room towards an attractive woman whom he assumed to be in her late thirties. Tall and slim, with long dark hair which fell softly in deep waves on to her shoulders, she was dressed in an obviously expensive dark green tweed suit. Under the jacket she wore a crisp cream blouse and around her neck a double row of pearls, their creamy sheen shouting out to the world that they were the genuine article. Both her hands were bedecked with rings, but the one that caught everyone's eye was a large diamond solitaire that sparkled and gleamed from every facet, as only a real diamond can.

Harry glanced appreciatively at her long legs. They were even better than Leo's bit of stuff, he thought. Harry was definitely a leg man. Underneath that unprepossessing, cold exterior smouldered a passion that had been stifled for years by Fran's remarks one night when he'd been unable to achieve results when fondling her mountainous flesh. She'd patted his buttocks condescendingly, saying, "You're getting too old, dear. We'll go to the library tomorrow. I've always preferred a good read anyway."

Harry stretched out his hand and smiled, showing yellowing teeth. "Allow me, my dear."

Alicia rose slowly and took his arm and the other three men, taking a lead from Harry Gough's old world courtesy, followed suit, each choosing a lady to take into the dining room.

The soup was eaten in complete silence, broken only by a hint of a slurp from Leo.

Maggie McCriel leaned back in her chair with a satisfied sigh, saying in a surprised voice, "That…was absolutely delicious."

Leo tipped his plate towards him and noisily spooned up the last dregs of the soup. "Don't sound so surprised. They can cook in Yorkshire, you know." His tone was belligerent, defensive of his native Yorkshire in spite of not having lived there for many years.

"I'm sorry. I didn't mean to…it's just that…"

"She wasn't being offensive, old chap." Her brother Tom McCriel leapt to her defence.

They were interrupted by the entrance of a young girl, dressed in a short, tight black skirt and white blouse. Deftly but noisily gathering the soup plates together she announced, "Next course'll be a bit late. Cook says to tell yer t'puddin's 'aven't riz an' t'gravys gone lumpy. So talk among yer sens for a bit. 'Ave yer finished, madam?" This to Alicia, who had barely touched the delicious, home-made mushroom soup.

James Brent interrupted. "I think my wife's not feeling very well. You can take it away."

"Cook'll not be pleased."

"That will do, girl." Harry Gough dabbed his thin lips with a snow-white linen napkin. "Whilst we await what I'm sure will be a culinary delight, shall we take the opportunity of continuing our introductions? Maggie and Tom McCriel. Maggie is an architect, recommended to Miss Maud by one of our senior partners. She will, I'm sure, be able to offer some constructive advice on the project. Tom, her brother, is a doctor, taking a short break away from his busy practice."

"A doctor," interrupted the speaker's wife eagerly.

Harry frowned at her. "As I said, Tom is taking a short break away from his work. My wife, I've already introduced. James Brent, a director of his father's building firm, also here through personal recommendation. James has travelled from Hertfordshire to be with us this weekend and…" he looked questioningly at the tall dark-haired woman sitting opposite him "my charming dining companion is…?"

James smiled at his wife and replied, "My wife, Alicia. Who, I'm sorry to say isn't really on top form this evening."

Harry Gough looked over the top of his spectacles. "Oh, I am sorry my dear. Nothing serious I hope?"

Alicia had been staring round the room. "What…oh…no. I'm alright. Thank you."

"And…*your* young lady, Leo?" Fran asked disparagingly, inspecting the girl and making it obvious she did not approve of what she saw.

The girl returned her gaze with deep blue, guileless eyes, smiling prettily and disarmingly at Fran. She knew her sort. And she knew how to dispel any fears she may have of her dallying with her husband. Pippa, knowing which side her bead was buttered, was strictly a one man at a time girl.

"I'm Pippa, Mrs Gough. Mrs Gough...I love that cardigan. Such a lovely colour. And so cosy for this time of the year. Perhaps you'd tell me where you bought it?"

Fran Gough positively glowed. "I knitted it myself. I can give you the pattern if you want."

"You knitted it *yourself*? I can hardl*y believe* it. I'm not clever enough to follow a pattern, I'm afraid."

Fran Gough, by now completely captivated by the pretty young thing sitting opposite her, leaned across the table and patted her hand.

"Then I shall knit one for you."

Pippa beamed around the table, triumphantly. She'd achieved her objective. Pippa liked to be liked.

"Lucy." There was a shout from the direction of the kitchen. "Get back in 'ere afore I skelp yer arse."

Harry, who appeared to have placed himself in charge of affairs, turned to the girl, who was standing with a pile of plates in her hands, listening with interest to the conversation and completely ignoring both the command and the threat.

"I...seem to think your presence is required in the kitchen, my dear."

"S'all right. She's me Muther. She's worked 'ere for yonks. Thinks I should join 'er."

Lucy slowly stared around the table, her eyes stopping at Tom McCriel, the youngest and by far the most attractive male in the group.

Smiling at him provocatively, she said, in a contrived, husky voice, "I've got me sights set 'igher than skivvyin' for pushed up gentry."

"That'll do, girl." Harry spoke sharply now and the girl moved sulkily to the door.

"Will somebody open t'door? *Please*," she added sarcastically.

"Bloody socialists," muttered Leo. "They've a lot to answer for."

Maggie McCriel smiled across the table at Alicia. "Are you from Hertfordshire too, Mrs Brent?"

"Alicia." James nudged his wife's arm and she looked up, startled.

"Oh...I'm so sorry. You were saying...Maggie, isn't it? Do...please...call

10

me Alicia."

"I said are you from Hertfordshire?"

"No. I moved from further south when I was a child, but I regard Hertfordshire as my home."

"Have you never lived in Yorkshire?" Pippa, twiddling a long, blonde lock between her fingers, leaned forward to look at Alicia.

"No. This is my first visit."

"Really. How strange."

"Why strange?" laughed Maggie. "This is our first visit too. Are you from Yorkshire, Pippa?"

"Me? No. Lancashire. But...I can't understand...."

"Ah, here's Cook. Now there's a sight for sore eyes."

The door was being pushed open by Cook's rear-end, reminiscent of a hippopotamus backing away from a crowd of hunters. Pippa began to giggle as she realized that the object of Harry's admiration was not the expanse of flesh now wobbling uncontrollably under the weight of the silver serving dish she was carrying, but the huge baron of beef sitting in the middle of it.

Harry rose immediately from the table to hold the door open and Cook, her face now crimson as a turkey-cock and dripping with perspiration, was followed by Aggie Brown, her set, wrinkled features disturbed by an unaccustomed, uncertain little smile hovering round her lips. Almost reverently, she placed a gigantic plate filled with Yorkshire puddings in the centre of the long, oak dining table.

"Are these yours, Aggie?" Leo's eyes softened a little as he explored the old woman's anxious eyes.

Aggie returned his gaze and their eyes held momentarily. Her tiny, taut body relaxed and the smile spread, lighting her face joyously.

"You allus liked yer grub, Mr Leo. Yes, them's mine."

She leaned towards him conspiratorially. "An'...guess what's fer pudding."

For a few seconds, Leo and Aggie might have been the only two people in the room.

The spell was broken as Pippa giggled. "I'll bet it's Spotted Dick and custard. He keeps trying to get me to make it."

Cook handed Leo a carving knife and fork. "You'll carve, Mr Leo."

The words were a command, not a request and Leo meekly took the carvers from her and began to slice the juicy, succulent beef.

There followed a long silence, not this time an uncomfortable silence, but one of total appreciation of the delights of real Yorkshire fare. The beef was cooked to perfection, the blood following the knife as it should, the Brussels sprouts offering a slight hint of resistance when cut, tender young carrots served whole and roast potatoes, brown and crisp on the outside, white and fluffy on the inside. The sharp tang of homemade horseradish sauce almost brought tears to the eyes of the uninitiated and the Yorkshire puddings, light and crisp, were accompanied by lashings of thick onion gravy. And to follow, there was indeed Spotted Dick and custard. Not the lumpy custard of school days, but a smooth rich sauce in which floated a pudding so light the diners gazed at it in wonderment that such a large lady as the Cook, with hands like shovels, could have produced such an offering.

The meal was accompanied, not with wine, but with a cool, creamy, frothy Yorkshire ale poured from large earthenware pitchers into fine, lead crystal tumblers. Aggie and Lucy served the last course. Crisp, white celery, apple pie and cheese. Lucy looked seductively over her shoulder at Tom McCriel and her departing remark of 'apple pie without the cheese is like a kiss without a squeeze,' resulted in her receiving a clip around the ear from Aggie's bony hand. Leo, wiping the froth from his moustache, leaned forward.

"Well, Maggie…lass. What's tha think to that lot? Tha dun't get snap like that in t' south, ah know."

The replenished diners laughed appreciably as Leo lapsed into his native Yorkshire dialect, everyone relaxed and a sense of jollification filled the air.

....

In a first floor bedroom sat a woman, not yet in her sixties but prematurely aged, imprisoned in a body bent and twisted by the relentless progression of arthritis. Her mind, on good days razor sharp and nimble, dulled by the painkilling tablets administered by the ever attentive Aggie, struggled vainly to remember what had sparked off the memory of an incident, now in the distant past. The memory of a fearful scream. Of the thud of wheels on a staircase, followed by the agonizing realization that something dreadful had happened. But before Maud could unravel the strands weaving and twanging around in her head like taut violin strings, the pain-killing tablets took control and she slept.

Chapter Three

"They're lovers," remarked Pippa casually, as she brushed her long, blonde hair.

Leo, lying stretched out on the bed, raised himself on one elbow with difficulty. He was feeling decidedly...he searched the annals of his childhood for a word that would describe his feeing of having eaten too much. Stowed. That was it. A good old Yorkshire word. Aggie was right, he mused. He'd always had a good appetite.

"Yer eyes are bigger than yer belly, Master Leo," she'd say when he'd visited Bishop Grange as a youth. Had to give cousin Maud credit though. She kept a good table. Like her mother, his Aunt Sarah.

He turned his attention to Pippa. "Who are lovers?"

"That Maggie and Tom. The architect and the doctor."

Leo laughed. "You're a nutter. She's his sister, for God's sake. Put that brush down and come to bed."

Pippa placed the silver-backed hairbrush down carefully on the old satinwood dressing table and gazed around the room. Although a washbasin had been installed in a tentative attempt at modernisation, there the effect had ceased. The rest of the room and indeed the whole house was pretty much the same as it had been when George Hepplewhite had brought Sarah, his bride here in the late nineteen thirties. And when *his* father had brought *his* bride at the turn of the century.

"It's all a bit...old, isn't it? Pippa shivered. "A bit creepy really." She turned her gaze to Leo and began to laugh. "You look just like a porpoise lying there."

"You take that damn silly nightgown thing off and I'll show you what rare beef does for a porpoise." He began to growl, menacingly.

"Sh, Leo. They'll hear you in the next room."

"No they won't. This place is built like a bloody fortress. The walls are two feet thick."

He grabbed her by the wrist and pulled her down beside him. She giggled as he twisted the ends of his moustache like a villain in a Victorian melodrama.

"Scream as much as you like, mi dear. No-one will come to your aid."

"Leo."

"Mm."

"Are you asleep?"

He groaned. "Can't do it again, doll."

"No, listen. What would you do with this place? You know, if anything happened to your cousin? It'd be all yours wouldn't it?"

"Not much danger," he grumbled, fully awake now. "Maud's only 57. Just two years older than me."

"Yes, I know. But she's got arthritis bad, you said. Can you die from arthritis? Wish you'd shave that tash off."

"Can't. Might sap my strength, like Samson. Don't know. Don't think you can. Listen…what did you mean about the McCriels?"

"That was his hair, idiot, not a moustache. Did Samson have a moustache?"

"I don't bloody know, do I? You said they were lovers."

"Who…Samson and Delilah? They were, weren't they?"

"Pack it in Pippa."

She lay back on the soft, feather pillow. "Christ, this bed's lumpy. All right, all right," as Leo dived down the bed and began tickling her feet.

Clasping her hands behind her head she repeated, "They're lovers."

"Jesus, Pippa," he exploded. "Don't let anyone hear you saying that. They'll take you to court for slander."

"They are," she protested.

"How do you know?" He was curious now.

"I can tell. I know about these things." She tapped the side of her nose. "Don't worry. I'm not stupid enough to tell anyone but you. You can go back to sleep again now."

"The hell I can. You've got me going now."

....

Tom and Maggie McCriel stood outside their adjacent bedrooms and looked around. A door on the other side of the corridor opened and Fran Gough appeared wearing a bright red woollen dressing gown, her corrugated waves now incarcerated in a thick hairnet.

"It's a job keeping it right, isn't it?"

She patted her head and surveyed Maggie's short, straight blonde hair.

"You should get yours permed while you're up here. It'll be ever so much cheaper than where you live. Brighton, isn't it?"

Maggie smiled. "Saffron Walden, actually."

"Yes, well...I knew it was somewhere in the south." Fran put her head on one side and inspected Maggie's face, critically. "It would make such a difference to you, my dear. Look at Pippa's lovely curls."

Maggie opened the bedroom door. "Yes...I'm sure it would," she said seriously, trying not to look at Tom's grinning face. "Perhaps next time. It's been a long day. Goodnight, Mrs Gough. Goodnight, Tom."

"Oh doctor." Fran Gough turned eagerly to Tom. "I've been meaning to ask you about my back."

Tom sighed. "Not tonight, eh. I think I'll go to bed, if you don't mind. Goodnight, Maggie. Goodnight, Mrs Gough."

Fran was left alone as the two bedroom doors closed. "Well, really," she exclaimed loudly. Turning back into her room, she muttered crossly, "It's true what everyone says. Southerners aren't anything like as friendly as folks in the north."

Alicia shivered as she undressed.

"Are you alright, darling?" James Brent watched his wife anxiously. "You haven't been at all well since we came here."

"Don't fuss James. I'm tired, that's all. I'll be fine when I've had a good night's sleep. It...was a long journey. I'll take a sleeping pill then perhaps I'll have a dreamless sleep."

"You do that. Think I'll go back downstairs. See if I can grab a nightcap. Give you a chance to get to sleep. 'Night, darling."

James gently closed the bedroom door behind him and walked quietly to the top of the stairs. There he paused, worrying about his wife. He wished she would go and see someone about this dream. A recurring dream from which she awoke in a terrible state, sometimes taking hours to recover. He reflected on what she had once...only once...told him about her dream. She'd had to struggle to remember the details. James had held her hand as she sat up in bed one morning, her dark hair framing a pale, petrified face.

"Try darling, please. I'm sure it will help if you can tell me about it."

Alicia, eyes tightly closed, had spoken quickly, as if afraid the dream would be erased from her mind before she'd had the chance to speak of it.

"It always starts with my walking up a long, wide staircase. This is extremely pleasant. It's a beautiful staircase and I feel as if I'm walking on

15

air. When I reach the top, a door suddenly appears and I'm filled with a terrible fear that I know will get worse if I go inside. And yet…I have to go in. As I turn the knob a choking sensation comes over me and I can feel a heavy weight pressing down on my head. But still I don't turn back. As I enter the room, the air is filled with a sound made by instruments I can't recognise. It's a kind of whining, wimpering music. The room becomes filled with weird shapes swooping down on me, but never quite touching me. Not solid shapes, but vaporized moulds without features."

She'd paused and he'd dabbed her forehead as she began to perspire. "Go on darling. You're doing fine."

"The air's oppressive. I look up and there's no ceiling. The walls extend up into the sky, like skyscrapers disappearing into clouds. Still I don't leave. I know I can but I don't want to. I feel I must subject myself to a certain amount of terror before I can rightly leave it all behind me. The strange sounds become louder and louder. So loud I feel my ears will burst. The dipping and diving of the shapes become a frenzied activity. At this stage, I turn and walk away. As the door closes everything is back to normal. But as I walk away, I know I'll return, knowing in my dream that I want to return. What's it mean, James? It frightens me so. Will it never go away?"

James sighed as he recalled the hunted, haunted expression in his wife's eyes. He would have to make her seek help when they returned home.

He stood and looked up and down the corridor. It seemed that everyone else had retired for the night. There was only one dim light on the staircase, casting strange shadows on the pictures on the wall. All those Hepplewhites keeping watch. Watching him. The house was still, yet not sleeping. It felt…restless, as if waiting for…what? James gave himself a shake. Such fanciful thoughts. Not like him at all. Perhaps he'd eaten too much. Perhaps he was abusing Maud Hepplewhite's hospitality by searching for a drink. He turned to go back to the bedroom but as he did, a voice rang out from the bottom of the staircase.

"Well…are you coming down or not?"

The hairs on the back of his neck tingled and he felt a childish urge to run.

"You're looking for a drink, aren't you?"

He peered down the stairs and as his eyes became accustomed to the darkness, he could just make out a wheelchair at the bottom of the stairs. Slowly, he walked down.

"I…do apologise. It's…Miss Maud, isn't it? Are you feeling any better?"

"I'll survive. Come on. You can get a drink for me as well."

James followed her as she wheeled herself into the sitting room. The dying embers of the fire still glowed, throwing a little light into the room.

"Don't put the lights on. I like it like this. Cabinet's over there. I'll have a whisky. A large one. No water. Then come and sit down."

Maud's voice was strong, authoritative. No one would pull the wool over this woman's eyes. Not, he hastened to add to himself, that anyone was here to do that. Peering into the drinks cabinet, he found a bottle of Famous Grouse and poured two generous measures into crystal glass tumblers, taken by surprise at the heaviness of them. This was…or had been…a quality household. He was not aware of the state of the Hepplewhite's present finances, but he assumed that the family fortunes had been eroded at some stage and that was the reason for Miss Maud deciding to dispose of the property. But the state of Hepplewhite fortunes was none of his business. His task here was to listen to any suggestions put forward and to give a rough estimate of the cost of whatever project was decided upon. His firm did, of course, hope to be involved in some of the building work, even though it would be a long way from base. All that would have to be taken into account in the estimates. And he was hoping a change of scenery would be good for Alicia.

James was very familiar with Yorkshire, particularly South Yorkshire, from his many visits to family. He'd often tried to persuade Alicia to take a holiday in the north, but she'd always pooh-poohed the idea, saying she'd no intention of 'clod-hopping knee deep in turnips'.

James had roared with laughter, saying, "Now there's a Yorkshire expression if ever I heard one. Where on earth did you pick that up from?"

Alicia had waved her hand, vaguely. "Oh, I don't know. Probably Emmerdale."

"Well, young man. How's your father, these days?"

James placed her drink on a well polished mahogany tripod table beside her wheelchair and sat on one of the leather seats, which formed part of the brass fender surrounding the fireplace, appreciative of the warmth on his face from the still hot, charcoaled logs.

"Oh, he's well, thank you Miss Maud. He sends his regards."

"Does he now? And I suppose he also expects to make a pretty penny out of me. He used to come sniffing around Bishop Grange when Grace and me were lassies."

James laughed. "I'll bet you were bonnie lassies too."

"Aye well, that's as may be. Not so bonny now though, eh?"

James sipped the golden liquor, savouring its smoothness. "Well he'd be sorry to see you suffering like this, that's for sure. He tells me your mother, Sarah, was also affected."

"Yes."

Maud answered brusquely, making it clear that she did not want to discuss the matter. An uneasy silence followed, with James racking his brains to find conversation that would not offend.

"My father is most grateful Miss Maud, for your having thought of him for this job."

"I don't do anyone any favours, young man, when it comes to business. Your firm comes to me highly recommended, but if you don't come up to scratch I shall find someone else. Is he not busy then?"

"Reasonably so. The housing market's a bit slow in Hertfordshire, as it is everywhere."

"And does your father like living in the south?"

James laughed. "He'd come back north tomorrow Miss Maud, if my mother would move. He's still a brickie at heart, you know. He often takes his jacket off and joins the lads on site. Says it keeps his feet firmly fixed on the ground. My mother despairs of him sometimes."

"And you? Would that wife of yours come to live up north?"

James remained silent. He sincerely hoped Miss Maud would not put that question to Alicia. His wife was not one to mince her words and if Miss Maud antagonized her, he knew she would leave their host in no doubt of her antipathy...entirely misplaced in James' opinion...towards the north.

Maud sipped her whisky, holding the glass with some difficulty. She winced with pain as she tried to replace the glass on the table, but James knew he musn't offer to help her. Life could be so unfair, he thought. She looked so old and yet, she was only in her late fifties. On the other hand his father, probably six or seven years older, was as fit and agile as most of his builders.

"So...what do you have in mind for the old homestead, James?"

"Don't really know yet. We're hoping to have a site meeting in the morning. I'm looking forward to seeing the estate. My father waxes lyrically about it when he's in the mood."

Maud snorted derisively, "You mean when he's drunk."

James smiled. "I think you know my father well, madam."

"I did. Once. So...let's hear what you intend doing?"

"Maggie has some ideas she wants to put forward."

"Ah yes. Maggie. The brother and sister act."

She spoke scathingly and James's senses sharpened.

"Act?" He looked at her quizzically, seeking further enlightenment.

"Never you mind. That's a pretty wife you have. You're just like your dad. He always had an eye for a shapely leg."

James looked puzzled. "But...you haven't met Alicia yet."

"Alicia." Maud repeated the name slowly. "Pretty name too. No, I haven't met her. But I've seen her. Seen all of you. Watched you arriving from my bedroom window. And that silly cousin of mine, Leo." She spat the name out, vehemently. "Whoever heard of a Yorkshire man called Leo. He should have been called Ernest, after his dad. Leo divorced his wife, you know. I don't hold with divorce. Marriage is for life. And that little girl he's brought with him. Young enough to be his daughter. I don't approve of Bishop Grange being used for immoral purposes. It'll bring God's wrath on to the house. Yes...I watched you all arrive."

Her eyes started to close and James, finishing his drink, rose to leave but her eyes shot open again.

"And don't think you're having that site meeting in the morning. You're all going to church. Everyone in this house goes to church on Sunday mornings. I'm off to bed now."

"Can I help you Miss Maud?"

"Certainly not," she replied spiritedly. "That's Aggie's job. She'll be around somewhere. Off you go to bed."

James rose obediently, bidding her goodnight. He climbed the stairs, slowly gazing at each Hepplewhite portrait. The Hepplewhite eyes stared back at him, each turning and watching him as he passed. He shivered as he thought of the woman he'd just left, observing them all arriving from her window. Bent and crippled, but with eyes as black and piercing as the ones he was passing. Not dull though, as were the portrait's eyes, but bright and perceptive. And there was another expression there. One he couldn't fathom. He shrugged off a feeling of approaching doom. Everything would look different in the morning. He groaned as he remembered they were all expected to go to church. Alicia would not be pleased.

Chapter Four

All the guests at Bishop Grange, with the exception of Leo, were anticipating being able to wander down to breakfast at leisure. They had visions of the old mahogany sideboard being laden with rows of gleaming, silver dishes and of lifting lids to help themselves to delicate morsels of kidney, bacon and other tempting delights. All the guests, with the exception of Leo, vacated their beds at exactly the same time. Maud, that most punctilious of human beings was, in spite of her crippling disability, an early riser and expected...no...demanded that anyone staying under her roof would do the same.

Lucy, the rebellious and belligerent daughter of Cook, had been assigned the task of dinging the breakfast gong, a task she undertook with malicious pleasure. Like Maud, albeit for different reasons, Lucy was of the opinion that because she had to be out of her bed, everyone should be out of bed. There was nothing servile about Lucy. At seven-o-clock sharp, Lucy approached the well-polished copper gong, housed in its deep, red mahogany frame, with a wicked gleam in her eye. Grasping the hammer firmly in both hands, she struck the gong a ferocious blow. For a split second the gong remained silently aghast, then responded with delight by delivering its message throughout the house, in an inimitable deep, rich copper voice, the far-reaching tones reverberating long after the initial strike.

Harry Gough, alarmed, leapt out of bed with surprising agility, his blue striped pyjama bottoms slipping down, revealing snow-white underpants. Fran had insisted he keep them on, saying it was sure to be cold during the night. Fran, who'd vacated her bed with a little more difficulty, but still much faster than usual, was resplendent in a pink, flannelette nightgown which had ridden up and beyond her hips, coming to rest on the shelf of dimpled fat. She'd felt it necessary to wear the cardigan that Pippa had facetiously admired the previous evening. The whole ensemble was topped with the thick hairnet, now slightly askew.

"What was that?" she asked with quivering lips.

She lifted one of her heavy breasts and scratched the flesh beneath it. Harry, realizing that the sound was nothing more than a call to breakfast, viewed her sadly. The picture his wife presented to him did nothing to aid his diminishing libido.

Maggie McCriel had been lying awake for sometime before seven and rose with relief. The eiderdown mattress was far too soft for her and thoughts of what species of insect life could be lurking within the feathery depths was making her flesh creep. She wondered if Tom was awake yet. He wouldn't be happy either with the soft mattress. She wondered if she dare go to his room. Just for a chat. Better not. There were bound to be people starting to wander around, searching for a free bathroom. What a mess this house was. Her trained architect's mind began to take flights of fancy as she pondered on how she would re-design the three hundred year old house, without destroying its character. She sighed. Tom would love a place like this. So would she. Away from prying eyes. Slipping out of cream silk pyjamas, she filled the tiny wash-hand basin with lukewarm water and washed quickly, then pulled on a pair of corduroy trousers and a thick woolen sweater. It was sure to be cold at the site meeting this morning.

James awoke with a start as Alicia stumbled out of bed. In spite of having taken a sleeping pill, the noise of the gong had awakened her immediately. James quickly swung his legs out of bed.

"You alright darling?" he inquired anxiously.

"I'm fine. What the hell was that?"

"What was what? Oh...the gong. It's a monster," he laughed. "Didn't you see it in the hall? You sure you're OK. now?"

"Oh, I slept really well. I feel great. I think I'm going to enjoy this trip after all."

James gave a sigh if relief. "Good. Listen...er...Alicia...Miss Maud is expecting all of us to go to church this morning."

"OK."

He stared at her, taken aback by her acquiescence. "You don't mind?"

"Naw. I've been a bit of a pain in the ass since we arrived. I'll try and make it up."

Pippa sprang out of bed with a shriek and Leo roared with laughter. Because of visits in his younger days, he was well acquainted with the early morning procedure at Bishop Grange and had been lying awake, waiting for Pippa's reaction to her rude awakening.

"What is it?" She gasped and shivered as the seemingly arctic temperature of the room hit her.

Leo's licentious eyes wandered hungrily over Pippa's young body. The sight of her long, swan-like neck, perfectly shaped breasts pointing perkily and provocatively towards him, tiny waist and rounded hips was incentive enough for him to risk incurring cousin Maud's wrath at what would be their late arrival at the breakfast table. Grabbing her arm, he pulled her back into the warmth of the bed. Pippa giggled as they were both enveloped in the softness of the feather mattress. There was nothing diminishing about Leo's libido.

Maud was already seated at the head of the table when her guests began to make their way down the stairs. Aggie, stationed at the kitchen door, looked straight ahead as each one entered the room, catching no-one's eye. Aggie had been well versed in apparent deference.

There were two empty chairs. Maud tapped the table impatiently with her stick. No one spoke. Harry coughed nervously. James felt he was back at boarding school, where conversation before a meal had been frowned upon. "I'll gi'em a call." Aggie made a move towards the door.

"No," snapped Maud. "If they're not down in two minutes, they'll do without."

As she spoke, the door burst open and Pippa sailed in, smiling disarmingly at the world in general.

"We're not late, are we?" she asked apologetically, daintily slipping onto one of the vacant chairs.

"No," smiled Fran Gough.

"Yes," barked Maud.

"Oh dear. I'm so sorry." She turned and looked her host squarely in the face. "Your beds are so comfy, Miss Maud. I just *couldn't* drag myself out."

The girl searched Maud's face, her deep cornflower blue eyes pleading for forgiveness, but the stern features remained rigid and Pippa turned away to find other, more sympathetic recipients. She was feeling more at ease with the company around her this morning and was desperate to chat.

"Ingratiating little bitch. We all know what kept you in bed," thought Maggie, seeking Tom's eyes. He smiled at her, as the telepathy between them mirrored their thoughts.

James watched them covertly, recalling Maud's words. By George, he wouldn't look at his sister like that. Wonder what the old girl knew? And...if they weren't brother and sister, why pretend to be?

Leo entered the room, rubbing his hands. "Cher..ist, its cold. It'd freeze the…" he stopped short as Harry shot him a warning glance. "Yes …well…sorry we're late. We…"

"Aggie…tell Cook she can serve," interrupted Maud. "There'll be no site meeting this morning till after church. The car will be here at ten. There'll be plenty of room for everybody."

Maggie and Tom exchanged glances and Maggie slowly shook her head.

Tom spoke firmly. "Maggie and I won't be going, Miss Maud. I'm sorry, but we're agnostic. It wouldn't be right."

There was an uneasy silence. Maud inclined her head.

"Very well. You must do as your conscience bids. Here's the porridge."

The porridge, thick, creamy and steaming hot, was served with golden honey, sweet as nectar.

"I've never had it with honey, have you, Alicia?" inquired Maggie.

"Mm. I think so, somewhere." Alicia frowned. "Although James and I always have salt, like the Scots."

"How are you this morning, Mrs. Brent? You're looking better."

Alicia smiled kindly at Pippa. "Please…do call me Alicia. I'm fine now. I took a sleeping pill and slept well. I usually dream a lot and that's quite disturbing."

"Alicia has a recurring dream. I keep telling her she should have it analysed by someone." James cleared his plate with relish. "That's the best porridge I've ever tasted in my life."

"Oh…perhaps I could help," said Pippa eagerly. "With the dream, I mean."

"What sort of dream, my dear?"

Alicia turned to find Maud staring at her. She tried to turn away but couldn't. Maud's eyes, coal-black, piercing, held her as if in a hypnotic trance. She opened her mouth to speak, but no sound came.

"What do you dream about Alicia?" repeated Maud, pleasantly.

Maud was smiling at her and Alicia gave herself a shake. She was determined, if only for James' sake to make a success of this weekend. He needed to prove to his father that his negotiating powers were as good as his.

"It's nothing, Miss Maud. Just a silly thing. James fusses too much."

"We have golden syrup on our porridge, don't we Harry?"

Harry Gough didn't answer his wife. He was trying to keep his eyes off Pippa.

"Ah, here's the bacon." Leo wiped his moustache with the back of his hand

and licked his lips in anticipation.

Aggie had already placed several racks of toast and dishes of creamy butter down the centre of the table. The kitchen door swung open and she and Lucy carried in plates piled with crispy bacon, plump fried tomatoes, mushrooms, black pudding, triangles of bread, fried to a crisp golden brown and on each plate, two fried eggs, their deep golden yolks wobbling slightly.

Alicia shuddered delicately as she thought of her cholesterol levels, but everyone, including Alicia, surprised themselves by demolishing with astonishing speed the most substantial breakfast they had ever seen.

"I don't know about going to church, Miss Maud," laughed James. "I think we probably all feel like going back to bed."

"I'll second that, eh Pips?" roared Leo.

Maud banged her stick loudly on the floor and Aggie appeared by her side. "Don't be late," Maud commanded. "Ten-o-clock sharp. Outside."

As Aggie wheeled her mistress out of the dining room, a universal feeling of relief swept over her guests.

"Right. I think we have time for another cup of coffee now…in peace."

Harry frowned. "You shouldn't say things like that, Leo. Your cousin…a most hospitable lady. She may seem a little…dictatorial at times, but she's very often in excruciating pain."

"That's a super ring, Alicia."

Pippa had been waiting for an opportunity to air a bit of knowledge she'd picked up whilst reading 'Readers Digest'. That and 'The Lady' were the only magazines Maud would have in the house.

"Did you know that the ancient Greeks thought that a diamond was a splinter from the stars?"

"Why…that's beautiful, Pippa. Fancy you knowing that." Fran Gough beamed at the smiling girl. "Yes, I think I'd like some more coffee. Does anyone want that?" She stretched out a plump hand for a solitary piece of toast. "It looks lonely. Shame to waste it."

"There's some lovely old furniture here, Leo." Tom turned to Maggie, smiling ruefully. "The kind of furniture we'd like one day, isn't it Maggie?"

"Yes. Goodness knows if we shall ever to be able to afford it though."

James listened with interest. They spoke like a couple just starting to build a home together.

"Your family must have been most discerning over the years to have acquired such quality pieces," Tom continued.

Leo nodded. "Yes. There's some good stuff. There's a Hepplewhite four-poster in one of the bedrooms."

Pippa looked puzzled. "It's all Hepplewhite, isn't it? I mean, that's Miss Maud's name and yours, Leo."

Fran leaned forward and patted her hand. "No, dear. He means..."

"You really are an *ignorant* cow, Pippa," Leo exploded. "Hepplewhite. The cabinet maker. You know...like Chippendale. And no," he added sarcastically, as Pippa opened her mouth to speak, "I don't mean those gonks that ponce around the stage half-naked."

There was an embarrassed silence at Leo's outburst. Pippa stared at him, her large, blue eyes gradually filling with tears. Pushing back her chair, she rose and ran out of the room.

Harry stood up, removed his spectacles and coughed. "There really was no need for that Leo. That...was ex*tremely* cruel. Excuse me everyone, please." He followed Pippa out of the room.

Fran stood up majestically, wagging an admonishing finger at Leo. "Harry's right, you know. Quite unnecessary. That poor girl."

She waddled out after her husband, her mountainous hips rising and falling with hypnotic equilibrium.

The silence remained unbroken. The old clock in the sitting room, at the other side of the hall, interrupted its monotonous tick-tock by striking a melancholy nine thirty, reminding Alicia and James that it was time to make a move if they were not to incur Maud's displeasure. It was with ill-disguised relief that everyone left the breakfast table to return to their respective bed-rooms.

....

"What do you think of the 'heir apparent', Alicia?"

"Leo? I think he's the most obnoxious character I've ever met. Do you know, I'm sure I've seen him somewhere before, or a picture of him."

"It's probably the portraits on the staircase. There's a distinct family like-ness in all of them."

"Mmm." Alicia shook her head, unconvinced. "She doesn't like me you know, James."

"Who? Alicia, you flit from one subject to another like a bee searching for honey."

She laughed as she slipped out of her trousers. "You're very lyrical this morning."

"And you're very sexy. Put them back on. Sorry to disappoint you. Musn't keep madam waiting."

"Fool. I'm changing into a dress for church."

"Who doesn't like you?"

"Miss Maud. That's why I'm changing. Don't think she'd approve of ladies attending church in trousers. I'm trying to get into her good books. I know how much this job means to you, James. I'm not going to let you down."

"You're imagining things, darling. She's not particularly affable with anyone. I think Harry's right. She's in constant pain. Here, turn round. Let me fasten those buttons for you."

"Thanks. You're probably right. Tell you what, though. I wasn't imagining things when I saw Tom and Maggie holding hands under the table. What is it with those two?"

James repeated to her what Maud had said the previous night. "I tried to get her to say more, but she shut up like a clam."

"Mmm. Odd." She smoothed the smart wool and mohair dress over her slim hips.

James nodded his approval. "Yes, that's better for a place of worship."

Alicia burst out laughing. "A place of worship. Don't be so bloody sanctimonious, James. You haven't been inside a church since we were married ten years ago. Seriously though James, talking of churches...I've a confession to make."

He looked startled. "What is it, Alicia?"

She paused for a second, lowering her eyes. "I'd never heard of Hepplewhite furniture either."

James lifted her chin and looked into her eyes. "Really? Alicia, what an ignorant cow you are."

They both laughed and hand in hand, left the bedroom.

Chapter Five

Lucy stood outside the bedroom door, covering her mouth to stifle her giggles. There was a shuffling behind her, but before she had time to make her escape she was dealt a stinging blow about the head and dragged by one ear away from the door. Aggie, in spite of her tiny frame, was as sinewy as a tiger. Young Lucy was no match for her.

"Eeow, gerroff me. I'll tell me Mam on you."

"You do that, me girl. And if I know yer Mam, yer'll gerra nother clip round yer lug ole, yer balmpot."

Years of serving a family that had modulated its accent to meet on equal terms with peers from other counties, had done nothing to temper Aggie's colourful vocabulary, often only understood by the indigenous population.

"That 'urt."

"Aye. It wer meant to 'urt, yer clarty little middin. What yer reckon yer doin'?"

"It's that Maggie. An' 'er bruther. They're doin' it. Ah can 'ear 'em. Go and listen yer sen' Aggie."

Aggie pushed her towards the staircase. "Get back darn theer. Wheer tha belongs. An' not a word to anybody."

Lucy ran down the stairs and, when a safe distance had been set between them, called back, "Yer wouldn't know whar it sounds like anyway cos you've never 'ad any, yer dried up owld prune."

Aggie, an inscrutable expression on her face, watched the girl in silence. When she'd disappeared from view, Aggie walked slowly to the end of the passage. Opening Maud's bedroom door, she crossed the room to the window and stared out over the long winding drive, her tiny, darting eyes for once firmly fixed straight ahead. Standing upright as a ramrod, her skinny arms akimbo, tight-lipped and with Lucy's departing words resonating in her ears, Aggie waited patiently for her mistress to return.

The congregation of the tiny church, built by the Hepplewhites in the mid nineteenth century to create an impression of being a truly Christian and charitable dynasty, had diminished alarmingly over the past twenty years. The two front rows were reserved exclusively for the Hepplewhites, but on this cold and frosty February morning, had it not been for Maud and her guests, the vicar need not have left his warm bed.

The spacious black Bentley was waiting at the church door when the party emerged. It had been cared for in its glory days by a liveried chauffeur but was now driven by the gardener who had been revving up the engine for the past five minutes in the hope that the vicar would receive the message and speed up his sermon. He bundled Maud unceremoniously into the front seat, anxious to finish his work at the house and get to the pub for his Sunday lunchtime drink before sitting down to his roast beef and Yorkshires. He'd no fear of Maud's autocratic tongue. No danger of him being dismissed. He knew how much she relied on him.

"I wonder, Miss Maud," asked James tentatively, having observed the narrowing of her eyes at the gardener's ignominious handling of her, "if we could be dropped at the gates? I think the walk would do us good."

"Can I join you? Leo, you don't mind, do you?"
Pippa, to everyone's surprise, had been at the front door at ten-o-clock sharp and, except for slightly puffed-up eyes, seemed none the worse for Leo's vitriolic outburst.

"I think I could do with a little exercise too," smiled Harry. "You can ride my dear." This to his wife, who'd been intending to anyway.

"Please yourselves," muttered Leo, ungraciously.

"Well, don't be late for lunch," reminded Maud, "and then you can have your meeting."

The four waited until the car had majestically proceeded down the gravel drive, then James and Alicia set off at a brisk pace, followed by Pippa and Harry, all of them breathing deeply, savouring the freshness of the morning air.

The drive was lined with an avenue of cone-bearing evergreens. Soft wood trees, pines and firs planted a hundred and fifty years previously to ensure a pleasing sight for future Hepplewhites and, of equal importance, to impress visitors as they peered out of their carriage windows. In its hey-day, Bishop Grange had been the venue for many gatherings and the Hepplewhite parties were the talk of the county. The family's pride and joy had been a couple of magnificent stone lions, crouched menacingly on plinths. These had been added by a member of the family who'd visited South Africa and this pro-vided the county with the gossip that, together with the idea of the lions, he'd brought back some unmentionable disease that the family dismissed as 'unfortunate.'

As the imposing facade of the house came into view, James observed an air of neglect about the place that he hadn't seen when he'd first arrived. Several of the wooden shutters hung drunkenly off their hinges. A couple of the long, casement windows had been broken and never repaired and the guttering, overgrown with weeds, had been allowed to fall into disrepair.

James felt some sadness as he stared at the old building. It was quite a stately, albeit small country house, built in the Greek revival style, its Corinthian columns boasting symmetry and proportion in keeping with the classic design of the house. But now it seemed somehow vulnerable, as if waiting anxiously to discover its fate. And his sadness turned to guilt. He'd some idea of what was in store for it. And he was going to help bring it about. He pondered on the history of the place. How it had been acquired. Perhaps Harry would know.

Pippa talked incessantly all the way from the gates. Harry smiled benignly at her almost childish chatter, but Alicia remained silent.

"You're very quiet, Alicia. Are you alright?" inquired James anxiously.

"Yes. But I think I'll skip lunch, if you don't mind." She laughed, humour-lessly. "I'm so full I think I'll burst if I eat anymore."

"Well, you and Pippa go in, Alicia. I want a chat with Harry."

....

"Yes James. I have studied a little of the origins of Bishop Grange, as far as one can. One has to go back to the enclosure and consequent privatisation of common land in the eighteenth century. Much of this land was acquired...or purloined, depending on one's political leaning, I suppose. My supposition is that it had originally been common land farmed by peasants and essential to their survival. You understand, of course, that I have no record of this. I would guess that it was in the Hepplewhite's interest not to keep records of their...well...removal...for want of a better word...of the small-holders. The Hepplewhites, along with many other powerful families would consider these unfortunates to be squatters and would have had no compunc-tion in throwing them off the land and turning them into paupers. Sad really."

Harry voice broke a little at this point and James turned away slightly, so as not to embarrass him, realizing with some surprise that beneath that cold exte-rior was a layer of warmth, along with a social conscience.

Harry coughed, polished his glasses and, having recovered his composure, continued. "And as I'm sure you will know, during the eighteenth century,

Britain was in a constant state of war. Regrettably the peace and prosperity which followed produced little benefit to the rural poor community. I suppose it merely widened the gap between it and the middle classes. I…was very fortunate indeed to belong to the latter. Now James, shall we rejoin the ladies?"

On Sundays, the main meal of the day at Bishop Grange was taken at midday. As they entered the hall, the aroma drifting from the direction of the kitchen indicated that preparations were well under way and, in spite of over-indulging himself at breakfast, James found his gastric juices being agitated in a most delightful way. Accepting Maud's offer of an aperitif, he sat back in his chair, breathing a deep sigh of contentment in anticipation of what he knew would be another delicious meal. If the hospitality they'd received since arriving here was any indication of what it had been when there were ample funds in the Hepplewhite pockets, then the gatherings here must have been lavish affairs indeed.

James settled deeper into the comfortable leather chair and dozed, dreaming of the days of splendour at Bishop Grange. He and Alicia arriving by coach for a weekend of fishing and shooting. He was dressed in deep blue velvet knee breeches and matching jacket with a white starched ruff at the neck and white ruffles on the sleeves. Alicia was resplendent in an ivory satin dress, and over her shoulders a crimson velvet cape with a hood. The coachman, who looked uncannily like Leo, helped them out of the coach with suitable deference.

"Sir James, Lady Alicia." He bowed deeply. "Their majesties have arrived and were asking if you were here."

As he spoke, the front door opened and the Queen, in the form of Miss Maud, a diamond tiara perched precariously on her head and carrying an orb, wheeled herself forward.

"Ah Jimmy. Phillip and I want you to ask your Dad if he'll re-build Windsor Castle for us. In Yorkshire."

As James was about to say they were too busy at the moment, but that he would keep them in mind, he was rudely awakened from his torpor by the sound of the gong, calling them once again into the dining room.

Leo, Maggie, James and Harry looked out across the acres of Hepplewhite estate.

"Well Maggie, if what you're suggesting could be pulled off, this could be a goldmine within a few years." James turned to Maud's solicitor. "What do you think, Harry?"

Harry took off his spectacles and polished them carefully. He coughed.

"Morally, I suppose, it's all wrong. But then, I'm here to act in my client's, Miss Maud's, interest."

James turned to Leo. "Leo?"

"Look…sod the morals. This is called 'market forces'. I want to get as much as I can. For Maud, I mean," he added quickly. "It's a bit of a gamble though Maggie, isn't it?"

"Personally I think it's worth having a go. There's no doubt that most of the council housing in the area has been sold off and there's no more being built, so there's a desperate need for low-cost housing. So although we'd never get planning permission for private building at this stage, the government have made it possible for land such as this to be used for low-cost housing and housing associations are desperate to find sites. After that…well…who knows?" Maggie shrugged her shoulders. "It's happened before. There's no doubt it would increase the chances of planning permission being obtained once there are houses on adjoining land, albeit low-cost housing."

Leo felt a wave of excitement rising within him. There was only one thing that roused him more than a young, firm, female form and that was the sight of his bank balance rising. His tiny eyes watered as he gazed at the land, his imagination working overtime as a cluster of exclusive and expensive stone built buildings sprouted out of the barren fields.

A sudden thought struck him. "Hang on though. If this low-cost housing is to accommodate peasants," he spat the word disparagingly, "how will we sell the land for up-market housing, eh? Owner occupiers don't want snotty-nosed kids with their arses hanging out of their pants living next door to them."

"Christ" fumed Maggie to herself. "I hate this man." Aloud, she spoke calmly and quietly. "It won't be like that, Leo. And anyway, the low cost housing will be well and truly screened. We shall plant fast growing shrubs around the estate. And in time, the tenants would be given the option to buy. So eventually all the houses would be owner occupied."

"Doesn't that defeat the object, Maggie? Surely that takes the low-cost housing out of the rented sector," inquired James.

Maggie shrugged her shoulders again. "Not our concern, is it?"

"And…what about the house, Maggie?" James continued. "What do you propose doing with Bishop Grange?"

There followed an expectant pause. This was the question on everyone's lips.

"It's...not listed. It can come down."

James heart sank. He'd had an idea that this was what was going to happen.

"Why, that would be bloody marvelous."

James viewed Leo with dislike. Had the man no feeling for his heritage? No feeling for history? To be delighted at the thought of demolishing a beautiful building like Bishop Grange was, in James' eyes, barbaric. Yes, it would be in his interest. If his father's firm were to be given the contract, it would be a feather in *his* cap...but even so...to knock it down and build...*what?*

"What could we put in its place?" asked Leo, excitedly.

Maggie hesitated, glancing at James and Harry uncomfortably.

"Eventually...a supermarket."

"What about a pub?" Leo's business acumen was now in gear, mentally listing which breweries to approach.

James groaned and Maggie smiled at him sympathetically.

"I know what you're thinking, James. But like Harry, I have Miss Maud's best interests at heart. From what I understand, she can't afford to keep this place going any more. And you've all seen the state it's in. It's falling apart. It'd cost a *fortune* to put it right. Then...well...ideally, she should only sell as much land as the housing association needs, wait till it's fully developed, apply for planning permission for the rest of the land...and then sell the lot."

"Well, *I* think it's a bloody good idea." Leo rubbed his hands. "I propose we go ahead."

"You don't think your cousin should be consulted?" asked Harry, mildly. "I don't wish to be rude Leo, but you really have no say in the matter. Miss Maud only invited you here this weekend because, as her only relative, she may wish to discuss it with you, but the decision does lie with her."

"Where will she go?" asked James quietly.

Harry turned to him with some relief. "Oh, she'll go into a residential home. There'll be plenty of cash for that. In fact, there still are some funds but they're gradually being eroded. The farm, as you have seen, is not producing any income. The fields have lain fallow for many years and the dairy herd was sold when Maud's mother died. All that's left from the livestock are a few chickens and geese. So the family's investments are barely covering the costs. In fact, there's very little invested now. Miss Maud's predecessors were inveterate spenders."

He did not add that most of the Hepplewhite males had died at an early age from alchohol related illnesses, having consumed with gay abandon most of the superlative wines and spirits that had been bought to be 'put down' for investment for future generations.

"Well, there you are," said Leo, triumphantly. "It's alright you saying it's got nothing to do with me, Harry. If Maud goes into a home, she could last for years. The money'll run out and I'll be lumbered with the bills from the residential home. I don't know what's happened to the National Health these days," he grumbled. "I don't see why I should have to pay."

"I think it's to do with something called 'market forces' Leo," responded Maggie, with sweet satisfaction.

Chapter Six

Pippa and Alicia were deep in conversation when Fran entered the sitting room. She frowned. She'd come to regard Pippa as her personal protégé. Fran had never had a child. She was one of four sisters, three of whom had been able to produce offspring with the apparent ease of rabbits. As one of her brothers-in-law had boasted, *his* wife could get pregnant from a sniff of his pants.

When she and Harry had first married they'd assumed that, like her sisters, they would have a child within a year, but it was not to be. Friends and relatives would still ask the pertinent and often hurtful question, "No children yet, Fran?" And Fran would not admit that neither she nor Harry were doing anything to avoid a pregnancy, and she would laugh, saying airily 'Plenty of time.' She'd lost track of the number of times they'd returned from an outing, upset and bruised by the insensitivity of acquaintances. Harry would go out again to his club, leaving her to curl up in a chair to consume a bar of chocolate or a slice of fruit cake, the sweet consolation mingling with the bitterness of hopeless, helpless tears. They'd vaguely discussed adoption, neither of them showing any real enthusiasm and eventually resigned themselves to a childless marriage, Harry throwing himself into work and golf. Fran busied herself with bridge, knitting and, without ever knowing what it stood for except that it kept the Socialists out of power, fund raising for the Conservative party.

"May I join you?" Fran pulled a chair towards Alicia and Pippa, forcing them apart. "You two seem to be getting along well." She forced a smile trying to hide her envy at the apparent intimacy of the two women. "Have you seen Tom anywhere? I want to ask him about my back."

"What's wrong with it, Mrs Gough?" asked Pippa, looking concerned.

This was what Fran had been waiting for. A sympathetic ear. She immediately launched into a detailed account of how she suffered and how men just didn't understand. Harry no *idea* what she went through. And he positively *refused* to massage her back even though he *knew* how much it helped.

Alicia leaned back in the chair and closed her eyes, leaving Pippa to contend with the predominantly one-sided conversation.

"Perhaps I could help, Mrs Gough. With your back, I mean," Pippa interrupted eagerly, during a break in the conversation.

But Fran ignored the interruption, only having stopped to draw breath.

At this point Tom entered the room and, on seeing Fran, promptly did a U-turn out of the door. But Fran, discarding Pippa, shot after him with astonishing speed for a woman of her gigantic proportions. Hooking his arm, she returned him triumphantly to the room, and wearing an expression similar to a hunter having ensnared his prey, led him unresisting to a settee. He scoured the room with a desperate look in his eye, but, finding no escape, sighed and flopped down on to the settee with a resigned look on his face.

"It's my back, doctor," she began, as if she were in a consulting room.

"Mrs Gough," he began desperately, "I *can't* discuss your back. It's unethical. Your own doctor wouldn't like it."

She opened her mouth to protest, but before she could say a word Tom continued, with an inspired suggestion.

"Tell you what though. I know this *wonderful* chiropractor who has worked miracles with some of *my* patients. I often use her. When I go home, I'll send you her address."

"He's lying through his teeth," thought Alicia with amusement. She opened her eyes and smiled at Tom sympathetically.

Fran looked thoughtful. A chiropractor. *Personally* recommended. Now *that* would be something to tell their friends at the golf club.

"Well…if you think it would help, I could try it, I suppose. I suffer so much, anything is worth a try."

"Now," began Tom. Having been let off the hook, he was happy to stay and chat. The site meeting was taking longer than expected and he was bored. "Perhaps, Mrs Gough…"

"Please, Tom. Do call me Fran. So much more friendly, don't you think? We're like that up here, you know. Don't stand on ceremony much." She was determined to emphasise the North/South divide.

"Yes…Fran…as I was saying…before we came…*up* here, I was speaking to a colleague who knew we were to visit South Yorkshire and he told me a most horrific story. It seems that, many, many years ago there was a terrible accident involving several young children. Fell down some stairs somewhere and suffocated."

"Ah, yes," she said, seriously. "That would be the Public Hall disaster he was talking about." She remained silent for a while, a series of expressions flickering across her face. "Yes…that was a sad day. It was a cinematograph show. You know, the pictures. My Grannie was there. Just a child, like the rest of them. I think they were all miner's children. Nearly a hundred years ago now. But folks here still cry. The King and Queen sent a message of sympathy. Sixteen bairns died, the youngest only four years old and the eldest, eight. Some blamed the parents for letting the little ones go, but…well…they did in those days. Still do, I suppose. I wouldn't blame them."

Fran fell silent again. Her companions were still, suddenly interested in what Fran was saying.

"Go on, Mrs Gough," whispered Pippa.

"They were queuing," Fran continued sadly, "to go up into the gallery. When it was full, someone at the top shouted for them to turn around and go back. And they did as they were told, bless 'em. But the ones at the bottom didn't hear. They'd be excited, you see. You know what bairns are like. Well…they fell. On top of one another. It was carnage, they say. The men, coming home from the pit, when they heard, they ran to the hall. Still in their pit muck, to see if *their* bairns were amongst the dead." Fran paused, her eyes filling with tears. "Their little bodies were piled four feet high."

Alicia stared at her in disbelief. "Is that really true? I've never heard of it before."

"Well…you wouldn't, would you? Not living in these parts. And it was a long time ago. It was in all the national papers, mind. But…well…mining folk are proud. Wanted to deal with it in their own way. Do their own grieving, without the country's prying eyes gawping at them. The newspapers were so insensitive. Just a story to them. No real feeling for the bairns…or the parents."

Fran's tears spilled over, trickling unchecked down her plump cheeks.

For a long while, her listeners remained silent, unsure of how to comfort this woman, no longer just a fat, little figure of fun, but a caring and compassionate human being.

Tom stood up, resolutely. "Go and put something warm on, Fran," he said gently. "You and me'll take a walk in the garden and you can tell me all about your back."

………………………

Lucy stuck a finger in a bowl of cream, scooped out a dollop and licked it. "An you can just go an' wash yer 'ands, young lady."

Lucy, completely ignoring her mother's command, continued to arrange salmon and cucumber sandwiches in neat piles on an oval, Moorcroft charger. Her dark, shining, straight hair, cut into a neat fringe and short bob on her mother's instructions…'I can't be doin' wi' 'air all over the place where food is'…suited her well. If Lucy had been born into a higher social class she'd have been considered a beauty, with her dark brown eyes, surrounded by long, black lashes, pale complexion and generous mouth. And she would have been referred to as having delightful and exquisite elfin proportions. Unfortunately her background, plus her financial position and occupation, decreed that she be classified as belonging in the D box and she was described by her peers as anaemic, skinny and having a big gob.

"It's a shame ter cuvver them lovely pomegranates painted on this plate. If these plates were mine, I'd 'ave 'em on a shelf to show 'em off." Lucy ran her fingers admiringly round the edge of the charger.

"Well, th' not yourn, so gerrum filled wi grub. Then cut up them cakes. An' don't be pinchin' any o' that fruit cake. Yer can 'ave a bit of that seed cake if yer 'ungry. Eee…I can't wait to get me feet up."

Cook had had a busy day and was in no mood to listen to her daughter's chatter. She liked Sundays. Because the main meal was taken at midday, as soon as tea had been served in the afternoon she was free.

"Mam." Lucy sat down suddenly. "Mam…do you remember the 'iggin-bottoms? They lived in yon end cottage."

Cook deftly split a lemon sponge and, with a practiced movement, quickly spread a layer of thick cream on one side and sandwiched the two pieces together.

"Course I do. Rum lot, the lads were. Ellen war a pal o' yourn, weren't she? I remember 'er Mam dyin'. An' then that poor young lass were left to fend for 'er Father and them three brothers. 'Ard working family they were, mind yer'. But it were too much forra young lass ter cope wi'. An' they paid 'er nowt fer fettling' for 'em. Typical farmers. Owd 'igginbottom war as tight as a knat's arse when it came ter spending brass. Ah seem ter remember she 'opped it an' went ter work in a boozer. What made yer think o' them all of a sudden?"

Lucy remained silent, unsure whether to continue.

"Cum on. Finish them sandwiches. They'll all be back soon, 'ungry enough to eat a scabby bairn. There's not enough there, lass. Mr Leo'll eat them 'is sen."

"I dun't like 'im, Mam. Ees brussen. An'…'e pinched me bum yesterday."

I dun't know 'ow that Pippa can bear to let 'im touch 'er. Listen Mam. Abaht Ellen. Yer remember Ben, 'er youngest brother? 'E tried to tup 'er."

Cook stopped her culinary tasks. Holding the palette knife in mid air, she stared at her daughter in disbelief.

"What yer mean, Lucy?"

"Yer know, Mam. 'Eed bin mekin' bramble wine. Drank too much of it one night and bust into Ellen's bedroom. Jumped into bed wi' 'er."

"Gerraway," breathed her mother. "Yer niver telt me this afore. An'...did 'e?"

"Nearly," nodded Lucy, energetically. "But Ellen's a big lass, in't she? She fought 'im off. The other lads 'eard commotion and dragged 'im off 'er. Gave 'im a bloody good 'idin' so Ellen said. Their Dad wor out late, so 'e knew nowt abaht it. They all decided not to say owt to 'im. Cos yer know, Mam, if eed've found out, 'e would've shoved 'is shot gun up Ben's arse an' blown 'is eyeballs out."

In spite of herself, Cook began to laugh helplessly at her girl's lurid description of what would have been in store for the over amorous Ben.

"It's called incest, yer know."

"I know what it's called," said her mother, cutting her laughter short. "And that's enough o' that kind o' gab from you."

"But Mam, that's what *they're* doin'. That Maggie an' Tom. He's 'er brother. An' she's 'is sister."

Her mother sat down and pummelled her chest. "Ee lass, that's browt on me palpitations. Now listen to me, me girl. 'Ave yer told any wun else abawt this?"

"Only Aggie, Mam."

"Listen Lucy. 'Ave worked in big 'ouses a long time. The's lots o' things that 'appen. Yer just close yer eyes an' say nowt if yer want ter keep yer job. Just you forget it an'keep yer gob shut in future. Yer see, Lucy luv, there's never been a truer sayin' than there's nowt ser queer as folk."

....

"Fran's a good sort isn't she, Alicia?" Pippa kicked off her shoes and held out a dainty foot to the fire. "Do you think she and Harry are happy?"

"I really don't know, Pippa. Why do you ask?"

"No reason. It's just that…they're both such nice people, but…as a couple, they don't seem to…well…*gel*."

Alicia, feeling warm, relaxed and in a mood for pleasant, undemanding conversation, smiled at the girl's serious expression.

"They must have…*gelled* at one time, Pippa. I suppose that couples can grow apart after a while. And with Harry being a professional man, probably with a busy social life and Fran staying at home to look after the kids, they ceased to have a great deal in common."

"Oh no, they don't have any children. If they had…" Pippa stopped and inspected her painted toenails critically. "I *must* do my nails. They're looking *dreadful*."

"You were saying, Pippa?" prompted Alicia.

"Mmm?" Pippa leaned forward to inspect the offending nails closer.

"No children. Fran and Harry. You were saying if they had."

"Was I? I can't remember what I was going to say now. You and James gel. You look made for each other. Are you still in love with him? He adores you."

"Is it so obvious?"

Pippa nodded and gazed at Alicia with childish innocence. Alicia smiled to herself, convinced that Pippa was not *quite* so naive as she appeared.

"*Are* you still in love, Alicia? Where did you meet? *Do* tell me. I *love* to hear about other peoples' romances."

Alicia laughed. "Well…I'm not sure mine's all that interesting. Usual stuff, I suppose. I worked in the office. At his father's building firm. I married the boss's son. I was the envy of the typing pool. That's all there is to it."

"Gosh. You did well. Are you rich, then? You look rich. Why do some people actually look rich, Alicia? No matter how much I spent on clothes, I would never look like you. You have style…class. You must have come from a good family though, to know how to dress well."

"That's enough about me." Alicia spoke abruptly.

She rose and walked across the room to the window, resting her hands on the wide ledge, her shoulders hunched and tense. Pippa watched her with interest, her big, blue eyes narrowing slightly. She remained silent, as Alicia gradually relaxed and turned away from the window.

"And…what about you, Pippa?" she asked, brightly. "Are you in love with Leo?"

"Oh, goodness me, no," she replied with delightful candour.

"But…well…he's generous. We have a good time, most of the time."

"And is that enough?"

Pippa pondered for a moment. "I've never thought about it much. Not until this weekend. But I have a feeling. A feeling that this weekend is going to change things. Don't ask me what, cos I don't know. Just a feeling......." Pippa stopped suddenly and placed a finger on her lips, motioning Alicia to be quiet.

Tiptoeing silently on her bare feet towards the door, she reached out her hand and carefully turned the handle. Flinging the door open, she was just in time to see a tiny, black-clad figure disappearing across the hall and into the dining room.

Pippa closed the door quietly and leaned with her back against it. Alicia looked at her, questioningly.

"Now *why*," mused Pippa, "should Aggie have been listening at the door?"

Chapter Seven

"I'm sure you're doing the right thing, cousin Maud," said Leo with a fatuous smile. He'd been in high spirits since Maud had announced at teatime that she intended taking the professional advice given by Maggie and Harry.

"Aye, well…you can take that silly grin off your face, Leo. If it doesn't work out as expected, you may well be stuck with me."

"And very welcome you will be Maud," Leo replied, in a voice as oily as a car mechanic's rag.

James squirmed as he listened, his aversion growing as he likened him to Dicken's Uriah Heap. "Dear God," he prayed silently, "please let Maud out-live her grovelling cousin."

Harry coughed dryly, removed his spectacles and polished them with a tiny chamois cloth he kept in his top pocket. They didn't need polishing, but Harry, as a young trainee solicitor, had been rather shy, often at a loss for words. The action had given him time to think and the habit had stayed with him, only now he only used it to give him a feeling of superiority. Kept his clients waiting for that couple of minutes longer. Made them feel just a shade uncomfortable.

"I too, think you have made a judicious decision, Miss Maud. As I said before, it is now a question of timing, although we shall proceed immediately with the application for low-cost housing. You, Maggie, will contact the housing association, informing them of our proposal."

Sunday tea at Bishop Grange was an informal affair, taken in front of a blazing log fire in the sitting room. Outside, the playful breeze that had been teasing and taunting the snowdrops had now manifested into its true character and was noisy and savage, lashing the winter cherry into bowed submission. But the shutters had been fastened and the heavy, brown velvet curtains drawn, excluding the sounds and the darkness of the cold February evening. Maud's guests felt able to relax now that business had been concluded to everyone's apparent satisfaction. The mouth-watering dainty sandwiches and tempting cakes were viewed with eager anticipation, without a thought of tomorrow and, for some, the long drive home. Maggie was reasonably confident that the first phase of development would go ahead with few, if any, problems and that time would take care of the subsequent plans. James felt sure that his firm would be given the contract for the low-cost housing. His father would be pleased with him and he could see a partnership looming ahead.

James' father, a self-made man, had tenaciously worked his way up in the building trade and, by the time he was thirty, was employing a hundred men. A much respected employer, he asked nothing of his work force that he wasn't prepared to do himself. He considered no job too big for him and was willing to work anywhere in the country. It was whilst he'd been negotiating the purchase of building plots in Hertfordshire that he'd met and married a local girl, reluctantly leaving his native county to settle near her parents, much to the chagrin of his parents and the dismay of the girl to whom he'd been engaged for the previous three years.

"Nowt I can do about it, lass," he'd told her, bluntly. "She's in t'family way and I won't let her down and that's that."

But moving away from Yorkshire had not rid him of any of his Northern traits and in true old Yorkshire fashion he'd dominated the household, ruling James with a rod of iron. The one concession he'd made to his wife on the upbringing of the boy was that he should attend boarding school and, away from the harsh rigours of home, these had been the happiest days of James' life. However, there the namby-pambying....the Patriarch's words....ended and when James left his blessed haven he was put to work on a building site to learn the trade.

When James had seen Alicia working in his father's office, for him it had been love at first sight. But...he wasn't always sure of *her* affections, even though she'd eagerly accepted when he'd asked her to marry him. But he often felt there was a part of her he could never share. A feeling that she was always on her guard, always holding something back. She'd a faint scar on her cheek, imperceptible to a casual acquaintance, but which showed up quite clearly when she was under any kind of pressure. He'd asked her about it once and, to his horror, she'd flown into a rage of such intensity he'd feared for her sanity. This outburst had been followed by a period of depression and he'd never mentioned it again. And yet, with his father, she was always at ease and his father adored her. So much so that he often felt a little jealous and he was sure his mother did too.

What Alicia would not do though was to comply with her father-in-law's instructions and James' desire, to 'give us a grandbairn.'

"Keep out of it, Father," she'd say, delicately tapping the side of her nose. But, for most of the time, they were a happy, united family and James was delighted that this weekend had been fruitful and would, in due course, contribute to the prosperity of the firm's already successful business. James was well paid, which was fortunate. Alicia insisted on buying nothing but the best and her father-in-law encouraged her, delighting in seeing her wearing all the trappings of success.

And so, contented, the weekend guests sat in companionable silence enjoying a second cup of tea delivered to them by a reluctant Lucy, her mother already having retired to her room to 'soak mi poor owld feet an' cut me corns.'

Pippa had removed her shoes and was toasting her toes by the roaring fire, whilst Maud looked on benevolently. She too appeared more relaxed, presumably feeling relieved that her future had been more or less settled.

"Will you be sorry to leave your family home, Miss Maud?" Harry Gough carefully sipped the scalding hot tea, frowning at his wife as she reached out for the last piece of fruitcake.

"Nobody wanted this, did they" she stated, taking a bite out of it. Fran had given up trying to lose weight. All her attempts at dieting had failed, mainly because she cheated herself by devouring cream cakes at every opportunity. So whilst registering her husband's disapproval, she calmly chose to ignore it.

"No, I shall not be sorry to leave. There have been happy times here, but it can be a cold, dreary house and, as you know, I have arthritis, as did my mother before me." Maud's coal-black eyes sharpened as she looked around at her assembled guests. "I saw my father and my sister die in this house and.....my mother was murdered here."

Her voice was so matter of fact, a full two minutes elapsed before anyone spoke, then Harry coughed nervously and slowly removed his spectacles.

"Surely not, Miss Maud. Surely... it was an accident."

Maud, ignoring Harry, carried on speaking. "It was the cleaning woman's child. Sweet little girl she was. My sister Grace and I saw her. We were coming out of the bedroom. My mother was in her wheelchair at the top of the stairs and she pushed her down. Mother died. The doctor said she was dead from shock before she hit the bottom. The child's mother knew that we'd seen. She came to us, distraught. Begged us not to tell. She'd worked for our family years ago when she was a young girl. She'd just come back to work for us again. Her husband had died in a mining accident and she needed the money. We felt sorry for her. The child was only about five or six years old. We knew our mother had been horrid to her and to the mother. Grace and I decided not to tell. I don't know why, except that our mother was

43

not really very nice to us either. And...she made our poor daddy's life a misery. What we didn't realise at the time, of course, was that she was in constant pain. Young people can be very callous, can't they? And...I know now what pain she endured." Her eyes clouded over and she blinked several times before continuing. "We never saw the child again, although we did see the mother once after that. At the inquest. And we kept our promise. Never told anyone. Not until now. Well....all water under the bridge, I suppose."

She held up her hand as Harry made to speak, indicating that the subject was closed and turned her attention to Pippa, who was sitting holding her toes, her big, corn-flower blue eyes widening as she absorbed the drama.

"Is my cousin going to make an honest woman of you, young lady?"

"What...marry me, you mean?" She giggled nervously, still pondering on Maud's revelations, the actress in her already creating a part for herself in the tragedy. She, of course, would play the frantic mother, appealing to the two sisters for clemency. She was concentrating on what she would wear at the inquest and had decided that a long black skirt, black boots and a flimsy shawl would be the correct attire and she'd scrape her hair back tightly, away from her face.

The question, coming as it did in the midst of her fantasies, caught her off guard. "Oh no. He can't anyway. He's still married."

Now, Miss Maud did not approve of divorce, nor of what she considere to be immoral behaviour under her roof, but she was even more intolerant of lying, having been brought up to believe that it was not only cleanliness that is next to Godliness, but also truthfulness.

She turned a frosty eye on Leo. "Is this true, Leo? You told me you were divorced."

Leo squirmed under his cousin's icy stare. "Well...I'm not *quite* divorced yet," he muttered, directing a baleful glance at Pippa.

"So...you're a liar as well as a fornicator."

And then Miss Maud dropped a bombshell of titanic proportions. To Leo, anyway. The rest of them, on hearing Miss Maud's pronouncement, silently applauded her.

"Harry. Tomorrow, you will arrange for my will to be changed. You're not worthy Leo, of inheriting any Hepplewhite money. You will not have one penny of it. Alicia my dear, Aggie is taking a rest. Come over here and plump up my cushion and then you can help me into my stair-lift. And you, young man," she said sharply, to a startled Tom, "will be in my room in ten minutes. I have something to say to you."

Outside the sitting room door, a slight, black-clad figure straightened up, then sped away silently, as the wheels of Miss Maud's chair came through the door.

The whine of the stair-lift jerked the startled company back to life. Leo, after taking several deep and noisy breaths, leaped from his chair and bounded across the room towards Pippa like a tiger going in for the kill. Harry, like the same tiger protecting its young, stepped in front of her.

"You stupid, ignorant *bitch*. What did I tell you?"

Leo lifted his hand to strike her and she cowered behind Harry, well aware of the intention that lay behind that menacing gesture. James struggled from the grip of a deep, leather armchair, still partly paralysed at the sudden turn of events from what had been a gentle, sedate gathering enjoying that most English of rituals…taking afternoon tea…to what was obviously going to finish in mayhem. He leaped forward and grabbed Leo's arm. Fran, with sudden surprising agility stood up and, bravely facing Leo, hit him in the face with her handbag. Caught off balance, he staggered backwards. Like a streak of lightening, Pippa shot past all of them and dealt him such a blow with her clenched fist, he fell to the ground. As Pippa's would-be protectors stared open-mouthed in stunned stupefaction, someone spoke.

"Can I side cups an'things away now?"

Amidst the confusion, no one had heard Lucy enter the room. Stepping non too carefully over Leo's recumbent form, she piled the crockery on to a tray and nonchalantly brushed the crumbs from the table to the floor.

"Is 'e dead, then?" she asked, conversationally.

Leo moaned and Lucy looked disappointed. "Pity. See you all in t'mornin'."

James accompanied Alicia to their bedroom. She'd returned from assisting Miss Maud pale and exhausted.

"I don't feel very well, James. If you don't mind, I'll have an early night. I won't take a sleeping pill. I'm so tired I don't think I'll need one."

James waited till she was tucked up in bed, then quietly closed the bedroom door and walked towards the staircase. As he turned to step down, he heard raised voices coming from Miss Maud's bedroom. He stopped in his tracks and listened. It was Tom and Miss Maud.

"I shall report you to the Medical Council, Tom. You'll be struck off. I'm warning you."

James strained his ears to hear Tom's reply, but his voice trailed away and there was a long silence. He retraced his steps back to his bedroom, but before he'd reached the door, Miss Maud's door opened and Tom, his face flushed, came out. He looked confused when he saw James and turned back into the room.

"Goodnight then, Miss Maud. I'll bear in mind what you've said."

He re-appeared, smiled at James and, without a word, disappeared into his own room. James went in to see Alicia to ask if she'd heard anything, but when he put his head round the door she was fast asleep.

Chapter Eight

Harry shivered as he poured two glasses of whisky and handed one to James.

"Put another log on, James please. It's going to be a cold night."

James looked about him. "Where is everyone?"

"Fran's gone into the kitchen to see if she can find any more cake. She gets rather hungry when she's upset," he added, by way of explanation. "And Leo," he paused and shook his head. "That poor child, Pippa."

James smiled to himself. It appeared that 'poor Pippa' was well able to take care of herself.

"She's taken Leo out for a walk," Harry continued. "Clear his head, she said."

James dropped thankfully back into the old armchair and drained his glass. "Dear God," he gasped. "I needed that. Mind if I have another?"

It seemed appropriate in Miss Maud's absence to ask Harry's permission. He frowned as he thought of their host, wondering what she had said to Tom.

"And Maggie....where is she? I was hoping to have a chat with her regarding the housing association."

"Gone to bed."

They each knew they were skirting round the subject of murder and of Miss Maud's imperious command to Tom that he go to her room.

"Can I fill your glass, Harry? It's a turn up for the books all this isn't it? Was Miss Maud's mother *really* murdered? Or is she imagining it?"

Harry handed his empty glass to James and shook his head. "I was just a young man when Sarah Hepplewhite died. A verdict of accidental death was returned. Her wheelchair, it seemed, overbalanced and rolled down the stairs. As far as I can recall, there was never any question of suspicious circumstances. I really don't know what brought this on. I do hope Miss Maud isn't starting to hallucinate. It could make future transactions very difficult."

"Well...she didn't seem to be hallucinating to me. In fact, she seemed to express herself with incredible clarity, considering it was...how many years ago Harry? Over thirty years?"

"Thirty six to be precise. Nothing to be done or said now though. Miss Maud made it perfectly clear that it is a closed book. Well James, I'll go and see if I can drag Fran out of the kitchen I think."

Harry sighed as he visualized Fran's hips increasing by the minute and quickly stifled a vision of a young, slim, naked body…and a pair of cornflower blue eyes smiling at him.

James helped himself to another drink after Harry's departure and sat debating with himself as to whether he should have told Harry of the conversation he had heard between Tom and Miss Maud. He shook his head. Best keep out of that one.

James awoke with a start. The fire was almost out and the whisky glass had fallen from his hand. Looking at his watch, he gasped. It was two in the morning. Must have dropped off. He'd been asleep for hours.

Feeling annoyed with himself for drinking more than his usual quota of alcohol, he rose stiffly out of the chair and placed the fireguard firmly in front of the dying embers. He walked unsteadily to the bottom of the stairs and there he paused, staring at the portraits hanging on the wall. They knew, he thought. They, with their ever watchful eyes knew whether Sarah Hepplewhite's death had been an accident or not. Slowly, with slightly drunken deliberation, James climbed the stairs, each picture he passed seeming to stare at him accusingly. Did they also know that he was going to assist in the demise of their home? James stared around him wildly, as the darkened house whispered back, "Yes, yes." He felt an urge to run. To escape those now reproachful eyes, but his limbs were heavy and restricted. When he finally reached the bedroom door he was soaking wet with sweat. And he was frightened.

"Come on, man," he told himself. "Pull yourself together." He held on to the wall. "It's the whisky. I've just had a bit too much, that's all. Alicia's right. Yorkshire's a God awful place."

As James entered the room, he spoke quietly. "Alicia, are you awake?" But there was no reply and he sensed that the room was empty. He groped for the light switch and moved slowly towards the bed, knowing full well she wasn't there. Immediately sober, he touched the pillow. It was cold. Panic-stricken, he called her name again, this time with increasing urgency.

The door opened and she reached out to him, almost collapsing. Her face was drained of all colour, its whiteness emphasized by her long, dark hair tumbling on to her shoulders.

"I've been in the bathroom. I've been sick. It's all this food James. I've never eaten so much in my life."

James held her close. "I was worried, darling. Get back into bed."

He undressed quickly and slipped in beside her, pulling her close to him. She was cold and shaking.

James kissed her. "You're not well at all, Alicia. We'll get away from here as soon as we can in the morning."

Her breathing was at once soft and steady and he knew she was asleep. But James could not sleep. His limbs were jumpy and, not wanting to disturb her, he carefully eased himself out of the bed and groped around in the dark to find his dressing gown. He thought he heard a noise outside and went over to the window, drawing the curtains back slightly, but everything was still. The trees and bushes assumed strange shapes in the cold moonlight. A barn owl hooted eerily and he shivered. He was not sure that he would want to live in a house, standing as Bishop Grange did, in its own grounds. A deep covering of snow had settled on the ground and as he peered across the lawn, he saw a fox step gingerly in to the white carpet. He moved the curtain slightly to see it more clearly and the fox stopped in its tracks. Looking up, it spotted James at the window and man and animal stared at each other, their eyes locked for a few seconds in nocturnal sympathy. Then, from out of the darkness, the fox was joined by its mate and the two set off together, trotting in unison out of sight.

Pippa lay motionless in bed beside Leo. If she moved, he might waken and if he did, he would want sex. Pippa never thought of sex with Leo as making love. She couldn't, she told herself. She didn't love him. She wriggled her toes slightly in distaste. Come to think of it, she didn't even *like* him. He turned over heavily and she held her breath as he heaved himself up on one elbow.

"Pippa," he whispered. "Are you awake?"

She lay still as death, scarcely breathing. He swung his legs out of the bed and went out of the door, closing it quietly behind him. Pippa shut her eyes tightly. He'd be going to the bathroom. She wanted to be really asleep before he returned.

And when Leo *did* return, Pippa was fast asleep.

If the guests at Bishop Grange had thought the breakfast gong's decibels were earsplitting, they faded into insignificance when compared to Lucy's blood-curdling screams echoing throughout the house.

Lucy had lived all her life at Bishop Grange but she still argued that as far as employment was concerned, she was only a 'temp', as she called it. Even so, both her mother and Aggie insisted that she conform to the harsh regime of being in service. Cook, her mother, had been employed at Bishop Grange for sixteen years, ever since she'd been dismissed from a country house in West Yorkshire, a house frequented by members of the aristocracy from time to time. She'd committed the unforgivable sin of allowing herself to become pregnant. She'd thought she was 'past it' and had become careless. So, at forty she'd found herself with no home and no job. In spite of having given the family twenty-five years of loyal service, she'd been unceremoniously bundled out the minute her pregnancy became obvious.

"I'm sorry Cook," her mistress had said, her tone belying the apology. "We really can't have any scandal surrounding this household. You know what I mean, don't you?"

Cook did indeed know what she meant, having very often been pestered by guests looking for what they laughingly called 'a bit of rough'. She threatened to reveal the name of the father, hinting that if she did a scandal would ensue but was told in no uncertain terms that if she did, there would be no reference for her. However, it was rumoured below stairs that it was the butcher who had left her with more than lamb chops and 'a nice bit o' kidney for yourself, Cook', on one of his visits.

Returning to her native South Yorkshire, she'd stayed with sympathetic relatives until the baby arrived and had then taken a live-in post at Bishop Grange on the premise that her remuneration would be lower than the norm until Lucy reached an age when she would be of use to the family

....

At five-thirty that morning, Maggie and Tom McCriel embraced passionately before Maggie left his bed, threw on a dressing gown, cautiously opened the bedroom door and peered out into the dimly lit corridor.

"It's all clear," she whispered. "Bye darling. And Tom...stop worrying. It'll be alright."

When Bishop Grange had visitors, Lucy's day began early and she also left her bed at five thirty. The freezing cold morning air whipped round her legs as she swung them out of bed and, prompted by the temperature rather than an urgent desire to commence her duties, Lucy dressed at breakneck speed before splashing her face with ice-cold water. She gasped as it stung her, bringing a rush of colour to her normally pale cheeks and she smiled at her reflection in the mirror before turning to see if her mother was awake.

Sharing her mother's bedroom was the bane of Lucy's life. Although Bishop Grange boasted many guest bedrooms, seldom used these days, the staff were still expected to sleep in tiny rooms situated on the third floor. Most of these were in a dilapidated state and Lucy had suggested that she could 'do one up'. But Miss Maud had refused permission, saying that she couldn't afford to heat another room.

"I need mi own space, Mam," she would complain when her mother put out the light. "I want ter read."

" Get ter sleep lass. You'll wear yer eyes out wi all that reading."

And Lucy would sigh noisily, saying darkly, "Wun o' these days…"

Cook was still asleep and snoring gently. Lucy closed the door quietly and ran down the two flights of stairs, ignoring the wide-eyed, ever watchful stares of the Hepplewhite portraits on the wall. Other mornings, she would take her time, stick out her chest, swing her hips and pretend she was making a grand entrance. This morning her only desire was to finish her chores as quickly as possible, waken the guests, help her mother to feed them and get rid of them. She knew there would be plenty of work to do when they had all departed.

After clearing the ashes from the grate in the sitting room, she re-lit the fire using screwed up newspapers, a few sticks and a little coal, bemoaning the fact that Miss Maud did not believe in spending money on what she considered to be non-essential items such as fire-lighters. This morning, the sticks were obstinately refusing to kindle and a very cross Lucy spent the next ten minutes coaxing life into the tiny reluctant flames with a pair of ancient bellows.

At six, the old clock in the corner of the room stridently struck a reminder that she was behind with her chores. Lucy pulled out her tongue at the inanimate but irritating vocal object, as a shout from the kitchen of 'Are you prayin' or summat in there?' alerted her that her mother was up and working. Giving the fire, now burning brightly, a final blow, she piled it high with logs from the estate, wiped her grimy hands down the front of the rough, hessian apron which enveloped her tiny frame and hurried to the kitchen.

"What yer bin lakin' at, girl? Go an' wash yer hands and get that table laid an' then yer can fettle t'sitting room. And mind and tek missus 'er tea afore seven or you'll 'ave Aggie bleating on. An' don't forget brown bread."

"What's she want brown bread for anyway?" asked Lucy indignantly. "As if we 'avn't enough ter do. She'll not starve afore she gets up, will she? She'll be 'aving 'er breakfast soon."

"Cos she does, that's why. All t'upper crust as a bit o' brown bread first thing in t'morning. It's ter move em. Na...you move yer arse."

"Well, I dun't see why...alright, alright. Am going." Lucy sped out of the kitchen, ducking to avoid a wet dishcloth hurtling across the room.

Pippa stood at the bedroom window gazing out on to the lawn. There had been a heavy fall of snow during the night after the wind had decided it was time to rest. Beneath an old copper beech, while snowdrops were still snuggling close to the ground, closely gathered around the trunk was a cluster of alpine snowbells. And to keep them company, a few premature yellow and mauve and deep purple crocus bravely poked their heads through a white blanket of snow, creating a tiny carpet ablaze with colour.

The bedroom was icy cold and Pippa shivered, pulling a flaming crimson and totally ineffectual negligee tightly round her. She glanced at her watch. Only quarter to seven. Throwing off the flimsy garment, she quickly pulled on a warm sweater and jeans, fastening her blonde curls back with a black velvet bandeau. If she hurried, she'd be first in the bathroom and could warm up in a hot bath. If Leo had drunk enough alcohol, he might forget that she'd hit him. He'd still be furious with her, of course, for telling Miss Maud he wasn't divorced, but he'd still want his nookie and she definitely was *not* in the mood this morning.

Picking up her towel and toilet bag, she opened the door quietly and, as she did, she heard a piercing scream coming from the bedroom at the end of the corridor. She stood frozen for a few seconds then ran to the room. Lucy was standing at the side of the bed clutching a cushion to her chest.

"Lucy," she gasped. "What is it? What*ever's* wrong? Are you *ill*?"

Lucy nodded towards the bed, her eyes rolling wildly. Pippa felt a shiver run down her spine as she turned and saw the grotesque figure lying motionless on the bed. It was Miss Maud. Her eyes were open wide, her cheeks grey and sunken, her mouth gaping and toothless. She was frighteningly still. Frighteningly dead.

In spite of her revulsion, the actress in Pippa rose to the fore and she could

52

once again see herself dressed all in black. Fortunately, it was her most flattering colour. She would be the distraught, last remaining relative at the graveside. But, as Lucy wailed like a banshee, Pippa came back to reality. She leaned back against the door, her senses reeling. She felt sick. Lucy was now crouching in the corner like a tiny, frightened animal. Pippa took a deep breath and moved closer to the bed. Reaching out a trembling hand, she touched Miss Maud's cheek. Another wave of nausea swept over her. She felt faint and, gasping for breath, swiftly moved away from the awful form. Turning her attention to Lucy, she gently cradled her in her arms, crooning softly as one would do to a distraught child.

"Lucy, Lucy. Hush now. Stand up and let's get you out of here."

She carefully propelled the sobbing girl out of the bedroom and as she did, other bedroom doors began to open.

Fran stepped out into the passage, her sagging breasts swinging from side to side like a pair of punch bags in protest at the unaccustomed effort of a quick change of direction from the horizontal to vertical. Opening her mouth, she sucked in a noisy breath of air but before she could say a word, Pippa handed the girl over to her.

"Look after her please, Mrs. Gough. I must tell Leo."

"Tell him what? What's wrong? Is the girl not well?"

But Pippa had disappeared into her and Leo's room.

"Leo. Leo, for God's sake, *wake* up."

She shook him savagely.

"What's wrong with you?" He sat up in bed, rubbing his eyes.

"Leo…it's Miss Maud. I think…I *know*…she's dead."

Leo lay back on the pillow and folded his arms behind his head.

"Is she, by George?" he said quietly. "Now there's a turn up for the books. What's that you've got?"

Pippa looked down. She was holding a black velvet cushion. "I…don't know. I think Lucy had it. I must have taken it from her."

Cook, who had been insulated in the kitchen from the commotion upstairs, bustled into the hall muttering under her breath.

"A'll *swing* for that lass o' mine, ah will. Where *is* she?"

Picking up the hammer, she struck the copper gong, if not with the wicked enthusiasm of Lucy, certainly with as much, if not more, force. Leo began to laugh as its boom echoed throughout the old house, his laughter mingling dis-cordantly with the vibrant tones of the copper like a musician racing ahead of the rest of the orchestra.

"The Queen is dead," he chortled. "Long live the King."

Pippa viewed him with disgust, the sound of his inane laughter jangling on her nerve ends. He swung his legs out of bed with a burst of alien agility and wrapped a warm woollen dressing-gown tightly round his bulky form.

"I'll slip to the bathroom. Christ, Pippa. I'm going to enjoy myself today. I'll show that Harry bloody solicitor and his big fat babe who's in charge now."

After he'd left the room, wearing a suitably lugubrious expression on his face just in case he met someone on his way to the bathroom, Pippa sat cross-legged on the bed, still clutching the cushion close to her, taking some comfort from the softness of the velvet. She stroked it absentmindedly, as one would stroke a cat.

"I just don't **like** him," she told the empty room. "I think...I'll have to review my situation."

As she spoke, something sharp stuck in her breast. Holding the cushion away from her, she looked down and saw a shiny object stuck to her sweater. As she moved, it flashed brightly and she stared in amazement as she realized what it was. Alicia's ring. Her beautiful diamond solitaire. Pippa stared at it in some confusion. How on earth had it got there? And then she remembered. Last night, Miss Maud had instructed Alicia to plump up her cushion and then help her into the chairlift. The ring must have caught in the velvet without Alicia realizing. She jumped quickly from the bed. She must return it immediately in case Alicia accused her of stealing it. Putting it in her pocket, she placed the cushion reverently on the bed, mindful that its owner lay dead a few doors away. Any other time, she would by now have created a part for herself in a courtroom scene, fighting to prove her innocence as the prosecuting barrister sneeringly pointed a finger at her, wanting to know how the ring came to be in her possession. But this morning, she had other things on her mind. Big decisions to be made.

Chapter Nine

James leaped out of bed as the sound of screaming filtered through his semi-consciousness. It seemed to him he'd done little else than leap out of bed since he arrived. He'd be glad to be home and resume a more leisurely approach to each day than had been possible here.

"Alicia," he whispered.

But Alicia was still asleep. James shook his head, amazed that anyone could sleep so soundly through all the noise. He reached for his dressing-gown, stubbed his toe on something, swore loudly, but still she slept.

James and Maggie opened their respective doors simultaneously. "What's happening Maggie?"

"Search me." She shrugged her shoulders, glancing quickly at Tom's room, but his door remained closed. "I think I can hear someone crying now. I think it's coming from the Gough's room. Oh God, James. There's a mouse running down the passage."

"There'll be plenty of those in this old place. Rats too, I shouldn't wonder. You're not frightened of them are you?"

"Terrified. Had one in my boot once. I nearly squashed it when I tried to put it on."

"A rat?"

"No, a mouse. And don't tell me they're more frightened of me. Heard it all before. Anyway, should we find out what all the commotion is or do we mind out own business?"

James hesitated for a couple of seconds. "Mind our own business, I think."

"I'll …just slip into Tom's room. See if he's awake. He'll be wondering what's happening."

James turned back into his room, wondering if that was all she was going in for. Giving himself a mental slap on the wrist, he turned back into his room, reminding himself to mind his own business.

"What's all the noise?"

Alicia opened her eyes and sat up in bed.

"Morning darling. You slept well."

"Mmm. What's happening out there?"

He was about to say probably a rat in Fran's room when he remembered that Alicia too, was frightened. He recalled her terror when once she'd seen a rat in their garden shed.

"Call Rentokil," she'd screamed.

He'd tried to reason with her that mice and rats are inclined to wander in and out of sheds at will.

"Not in mine they don't," she'd insisted firmly.

"I don't know what's going on. Perhaps it's Fran having the vapours."

"The *vapours*" laughed Alicia. You really are stupid James. Women don't have the vapours anymore."

"What are they anyway?"

Alicia yawned. "Your posh school obviously didn't encourage you to read Jane Austin or you'd have known what they were. James, I'm bored. Let's make an early start and get the hell out of here. And James…don't ever try to persuade me to come to this God-forsaken part of the world again."

"Ah…come on, Alicia. That's not fair. You haven't actually *seen* any of Yorkshire yet."

She swung herself lazily out of bed. "I've seen all I want to see. And heard all I want to hear. Get packing."

There was pandemonium in the Gough's bedroom. Fran could not stop Lucy crying, nor could she get her to say what was wrong with her.

"You'll have to fetch her mother, Harry. I can't do anything with the girl. Come on now Lucy," Fran coaxed. "Your Mam'll be here in a bit."

At this Lucy howled even louder and Harry, exasperated by this time, took her arm.

"Come with me girl," he said firmly.

"Harry," gasped Fran, in scandalized tones. "You're not *dressed.*"

"Talk sense, woman. How do you expect me to dress in front of this girl? Come on, dear."

His voice was gentler now and Fran beamed at him, confident that he would sort things out and she opened the door for them, sighing sadly. He would have made a wonderful father.

Harry marched Lucy down the stairs, through the hall and the dining room into the kitchen, where Cook was busy taking bread rolls out of the oven. He sniffed the air appreciably. Nothing like the smell of freshly baked bread.

Cook spoke nervously, alarmed at the sight of her daughter, now sobbing quietly.

"What yer done now, yer little bastard? And you, Sir. Why are you still in your pyjamas? *Lucy* …you haven't ..er …have yer…"

Harry quickly pushed Lucy away from him and shouted angrily. "For God's *sake*, woman. Look... I'll leave this to you, Cook."

Turning sharply on his heel, he left the kitchen, shaking his head as Cook said accusingly, "Yer've peed yer briches, 'aven't yer?"

Not being desirous of knowing the state of Lucy's underwear, he walked away quickly, head bowed and deep in thought, towards the staircase. Harry had important, unthinkable decisions to make.

Aggie stood straight as a ramrod as if on guard at the top of the stairs as Harry slowly ascended, head still bowed. He looked up as he neared the top step.

"Ah, Aggie. Good morning. How are you this morning? Be glad to see the back of us all, I'll be bound."

Aggie stared at him with unseeing eyes and walked past without a word. Harry shrugged his shoulders.

"Strange little creature," he mused. "But *such* a loyal servant." He reached the bedroom and was about to enter when Leo stepped in front of him.

"Have you sent for a doctor…Gough?"

Harry drew himself up to his full five foot four. "I *beg* your pardon, Leo? Is someone ill?"

Leo's face gradually stretched into a satisfied smile. "You don't know, do you?"

Harry looked puzzled. "Know what? What is it, man?" he demanded.

He pulled back sharply as Leo pushed his face close to him. "She's dead, Harry," he said softly. "Your client...is dead. And Harry...I'm the client now. Bishop Grange is mine. So Harry...be a good fellow, eh. Let's have a little *respect* now, shall we, Harry…old chap?"

The guests, each with their own thoughts, gathered together in the sitting room. Breakfast had gone ahead as usual. Cook, being well used to traumas in such households never interfering with the filling of bellies, had catered for a full complement, but only Fran, Harry and Leo had accepted a cooked meal. The McCriels, James and Pippa nibbled half-heartedly at freshly baked muffins. Alicia would eat nothing. Aggie and Lucy were nowhere to be seen and Cook, red-eyed, huffed and puffed in and out the kitchen. It was a relief to everyone when the meal was over.

James had brought their suitcases down from the bedroom ready for a quick get-away, Alicia having stated that she too would die if she had to spend any more time in this house.

Harry took a watch out of his waistcoat pocket. It was attached to a gold

Albert. James half expected him to swing it round and land it back in his pocket, as he'd seen a comedian do somewhere. Eric Morecambe was it? Or was it Jimmy Edwards? He gave himself a shake. The news that Miss Maud had died during the night hadn't quite sunk in yet, although the implication of what her death would mean to all their plans was gradually beginning to hit him. He was trying not to be selfish and felt a genuine sadness at her sudden death, but...he was concerned. He knew what his father would say if he were here. Business is business, that's what he would say. But the genes James had inherited from his father had been tempered by the genes of his more sensitive mother. He was having difficulty concentrating on business. His mind kept returning to the brief session he'd shared with Miss Maud in the small hours, with the rest of the house sleeping. They had been at one in front of the dying embers of the fire, enjoying together a last drink, which indeed had turned out to *be* the last drink for her. In spite of her outward crustiness, she'd looked so vulnerable trying to hold the glass of whisky in pain-racked, twisted hands. He'd tried to imagine how she must have been feeling, not really knowing what the future held for her. Knowing only for sure that she would become more and more dependant on other people. And with her independent spirit, she would have found that hard to bear. And now, he supposed, he'd have to negotiate with the invidious Leo, a prospect he viewed with dismay.

Harry frowned. "The doctor is taking an unconscionable time."

Pippa gazed at him, admiringly. He used such lovely words. Not that she understood all of them but he spoke them so beautifully.

"Yes, he is taking his time," James nodded in agreement.

"Well, we know she's dead, don't we. Tom really is a doctor, you know." Maggie moved close to her brother as she spoke.

"Well, he's the queerest bloody doctor I've ever seen," laughed Leo. "Wouldn't even go in to see her without you holding his hand, Mags."

Tom said nothing and there was an uneasy silence in the room as they all recalled that there had been some reluctance on Tom's part until Maggie had said soothingly, "Come on Tom. I'll go in with you."

James moved swiftly towards the door, anxious to avoid a scene as Maggie took a deep breath, obviously intending to defend her brother.

"Well...er...yes. I'd better give the doctor another ring."

"Ring," gasped Pippa. "Golly...I nearly forgot. Silly me," she giggled. "Alicia, I found your ring."

She dug a hand into her pocket and held the ring to the light. "See how it twinkles. It *is* like a star, isn't it? It's so beautiful, Alicia. It would have been awful if you'd lost it. I bet James would have been furious."

James smiled and took the ring from her. "Well, it would have been costly, that's for sure. Thank you very much, Pippa. Where did you find it?"

Alicia lifted her hand. "Of course. I remember now. I didn't have it on when I woke up, but I thought I'd left it in the bathroom so I knew it would be safe. Then, with all the trauma this morning, I completely forgot about it."

"You were very lucky, Alicia," Pippa nodded importantly. "It wasn't in the bathroom. It was stuck in Miss Maud's cushion. You know, the black velvet one from her wheel chair. You must have lost it when you helped her upstairs last night."

"Yes. Yes...of course. Thanks."

James slipped the ring back on her finger. "You really should take more care, you know. Father wouldn't have been pleased if you'd lost it. It was a present from Dad," he explained to no one in particular.

"Would anyone like coffee?" Fran made several efforts to stand up, but her legs were not quite long enough to reach the floor and the big leather armchair did nothing to assist her.

Harry sighed deeply. "Stay there, Fran. I'll see if Cook is still around. Is it coffee for everyone? Ah...here's the doctor now. He's sure to want one after he's seen poor Miss Maud. Perhaps we'll wait, shall we?"

Without waiting for a reply, he left the room and went outside to meet the doctor.

Another uneasy silence pervaded the room. Leo's unmistakable ebullience was embarrassing and Pippa viewed him with distaste. How could she ever have thought she could spend the rest of her life with him? Not that she had ever intended to, but her sense of theatre often dismissed reality and Pippa lived for the moment.

Alicia, warmly dressed in a green tweed suit and ready for the off, sat reading a magazine, pointedly ignoring everyone, whilst James stood at the window, gazing out on to the snow-covered lawn. He too, was now anxious to return home and report to his father. There was little else to be done here. He really felt unable to discuss business with Miss Maud lying dead in her bed. And...it would take time for all the legal knots to be tied. Could be months before they were able to even think about the development again.

"*Right* Jamie boy." Leo rubbed his hands together. "Where do we start?

Fancy a walk round my estate. I've a few ideas I'd like to run past you and Maggie. No good letting the grass grow under our feet."

Fran, spurred on by indignation, made a supreme effort, heaved herself from the depths of the chair and marched purposefully towards Leo, her short, pursy body shaking with rage.

Poking a finger in his protruding belly she said, in tones reminiscent of a sergeant addressing his new recruits, "You are, without a doubt, the most abominable apology for a human being I have ever had the misfortune to meet. That poor cousin of yours is lying up there, not yet cold and all you're concerned about is your inheritance. And ... remember this. She said in front of *all* of us that you weren't to have one *penny* of her money. And if she hadn't died when she did, you *wouldn't* have either."

"Fran's right, you know Leo. I really think you're being a bit premature." But as he spoke, James stifled an uncomfortable feeling that his father would have approved of Leo's business-like approach to the situation. He could hear him now, saying "No good having a deal stymied by a mere death, James. Life goes on, lad."

Leo smiled, unperturbed. "Do you now." His response was not a question, but a smug statement. "Well ... let me remind you that you are now...all of you...enjoying *my* hospitality."

Alicia replaced the magazine deliberately back in the mahogany Canterbury and stood up, galvanized into action by Leo's sneering remarks.

"That's it, James. I don't have to take any more of this. I'll see you in the car."

"Sit down, Alicia," whispered James. "We can't just leave."

"Ah, here's the coffee. Oh...scones too. Thank you Cook. I'm ready for this. You don't have a little jam, do you? And cream?"

Fran welcomed the diversion. She tried to avoid emotional outbursts. They left her feeling quite breathless...and very hungry.

"Now Leo." She waved a hand at him. "It may be your coffee we're drinking dear, but for goodness sake, try to be a gentleman and pour it please. And," she looked around at all of them, "has anyone thought about Aggie? Goodness knows how that poor soul's feeling. She's been here for nearly sixty years, you know." She turned her attention once again to Leo. "I just hope that you will be giving some thought to her, Leo. And to Cook and that child of hers."

Maggie and Tom had remained silent throughout the interchanges but

Maggie now stood up and smiled at Fran, indicating that she was in full agreement with her condemnation of Leo.

"I'll pour. Fran. You sit down. I don't know where...or how Aggie is. We *should* seek her out. She must be in a dreadful state."

"Come on in, doctor. I think we have coffee waiting for us. Ah yes...here it is."

Harry held the door open to allow the doctor to enter.

The doctor looked around for a chair. "Is there a straight backed one anywhere? I have a bad back. Can't be doing with these soft things."

"So have I, doctor." Fran turned to him enthusiastically. "A bad back, I mean. What do you take for it? Have you tried one of those...what did you call them Tom?"

"Chiropractor," sighed Tom.

"Fran ... *please.* Can we let Dr...er...the doctor get down to business. I'll fetch a chair from the dining room, doctor."

As Harry left the room, he caught a glimpse of Aggie moving swiftly across the hall. He had an uncomfortable feeling that she'd been listening at the door. Standing motionless, he watched her climb the stairs and when she reached the top he turned away, shaking his head sadly. She must be demented wondering what would become of her.

"Doctor, is it alright for my husband and me to go now? We have a long journey ahead. To Hertfordshire. It looks as if the weather could deteriorate."

The doctor followed Alicia's gaze as she looked out of the window. The weather had changed again. The skies were dark and gloomy and snow was falling heavily, the wind blowing it almost horizontally.

But he shook his head. "Dear me, no. I have a lot to do yet. My notes to take. The coroner will want all the details. This is an unexpected death. Although Miss Maud appeared old, she was only 57 and in reasonably good health. Her heart and lungs were sound. Of course, she suffered dreadfully from arthritis and the medication she took will have taken its toll. There is a price to be paid for every pill we take, you know. She was certainly of sound mind. A principled lady with extremely strong views. We had many scintillating conversations." He looked pointedly at the drinks cabinet. "And we had many a glass of port together on my routine calls."

Harry, returning to the room with a straight-back chair, positioned it by the blazing fire and walked to the drinks cabinet. "May I offer you a drink, doctor?"

Leo was out of his chair in a flash, beating Harry by a short head. "My prerogative I think, Mr Gough."

He smiled triumphantly at Harry, looked questioningly at James and Tom who shook their heads and poured two glasses of vintage port, handing one to the doctor and taking a sip from the other.

"Cheers doc."

Harry sat down, flushing with embarrassment and Pippa, catching his eye, smiled at him sympathetically before flashing a reproachful glance at Leo.

Dr Rodgers, unaware of any animosity between the two men, sipped his drink appreciably then lifted it to the light.

"Always did keep a good cellar, the Hepplewhites. Now, where were we? Ah…yes. No. No one must leave yet. We have to establish for a start who was the last to see Miss Maud alive. There will be an inquest, of course. Now, could I have everyone together please. Domestic staff included. I understand it was the scullery maid who found her."

Pippa smiled to herself. Lucy would not be pleased to hear herself described as a scullery maid.

The doctor, in spite of his protestations against soft chairs, had settled himself in one, ignoring the one that Harry had struggled to carry in for him. "I've asked Lucy to fetch Aggie," said Harry breathlessly. "Cook is on her way. You will understand doctor, that this has been a dreadful shock for them. They have…all of them…served Miss Maud with indefatigable dedication for many years."

Pippa stared at Harry with undisguised admiration. She made a decision. She would study. She would go to university. Study Law, probably. Pippa could see herself now in a black cap and gown, walking on to a platform, bowing her head as tumultuous applause thundered around the room. Of course, she would be top of the class. Other students would worship her, coming to her for advice, like in the film 'Educating Rita'.

"Yes, I do appreciate that, Mr Gough. Now, can we make a start. Who would be the last person to see Miss Maud alive?"

There was a pause in the proceedings as the door opened and Cook and Lucy entered, followed by Aggie. Fran inspected the old woman's face anxiously, but her expression was inscrutable.

"As I was saying, who was the last to see Miss Maud alive?"

There followed a brief silence, everyone looking around at one another.

"I suppose, Alicia, it would be you, wouldn't it? Miss Maud asked my wife to help her into her stair-lift," James explained to the doctor. "I presume Alicia, you went upstairs to help her out at the top."

Alicia nodded. "Yes. I helped her into bed. She thanked me, said good-night and I went to bed early. I must have fallen asleep almost at once and the next I knew I was woken by the commotion in the passage this morning."

She glanced at James and he nodded his agreement.

"Did anyone see her after that? Aggie, did you not attend to your mistress later on last night?" the doctor asked kindly. He had looked after the medical needs of the Hepplewhites for many years and knew Aggie well.

Aggie remained silent and Cook intervened quietly.

"She's in shock. No, she wouldn't 'ave seen 'er again after t'Missus went to bed. On a Sunday, Aggie's free after that. And…with 'aving visiters she'd tell Aggie not to bother seeing 'er to bed cos one of the others would do it see. She liked to give Aggie a bit of a rest when she could."

"So, Mrs…?"

"Brent," interrupted James. "My wife, Alicia."

"Yes…Mrs Brent. Then you will have to attend the inquest I'm afraid, as the last person to see Miss Maud alive."

"Hang on." Pippa stood up, excitedly. " She wasn't though, was she? The last one to see her, I mean. Miss Maud told Tom to go to her room. Said she wanted to see him."

"Of course," exclaimed James, breathing a sigh of relief. "I'd forgotten. You were coming out of Miss Maud's room Tom, when I came to see Alicia. You said you would take note of what she had said…or words to that effect. You remember?"

James had no intention of repeating that he'd heard Maud saying that he, Tom, would be struck off. That was none of his business, but he certainly wasn't going to have Alicia attending an inquest if Tom had seen her last.

"Of course," said Tom slowly. "I…had forgotten. It wasn't important."

"Right." Dr Rodgers was becoming impatient. "Any advance on Mr….Tom?"

"McCriel. I'm Maggie. Tom's sister."

"So." The doctor held out his empty glass, waving it at the drinks cabinet and Leo leapt eagerly to his feet, refilling his own and the doctors. "That brings us to who discovered the body."

Cook dug Lucy in the ribs. "Stand up lass when t'doctors talking to yer."

"Right…er…girl. Perhaps you will give us a run down on your activities this morning."

"What d'yer mean?"

Dr Rodgers sighed. "Tell us what you did this morning."

"I gor'up. Got washed. Got dressed. Went for a pee…"

"Oh…come *on*, girl. We don't want to know all that. What were you doing just before you went into Miss Maud's room and what did you do in there?"

"Well I was taking 'er tea, like I allus do afore seven. It were dark, see." Lucy spoke slowly and deliberately. "So…I laid the tea tray first on the dressing table in the dark an' then I drew the curtains an it were then I saw 'er. I went over to the bed, lifted the cushion off 'er an theer she were, eyes wide open. An I were that feart, I screamed and screamed. An' then Miss Pippa came in."

An ominous silence settled in the room as the implications of what Lucy had said penetrated the assembled group.

"Listen, child…"

But before the doctor could say another word, Leo leapt to his feet.

"She's lying. She's bloody lying."

"I think, Leo, we must accept that Lucy's veracity is not in doubt." Harry took off his glasses and polished them.

"Eer, what yer mean?" demanded her mother, rising swiftly to her feet.

"It's alright, Cook. Mr Gough means that Lucy is not a liar." Dr Rodgers smiled kindly at Lucy. "I want you to think carefully. It's most important that you recall what you saw without embellishment…er…without exaggeration. You understand?"

Lucy nodded. "I'm not daft yer know. I'm telling t'truth. She 'ad er black cushion over 'er face. I 'ad to lift it off ter see 'er. An' I know what that means. That's why I've bin so upset. It's not very nice…knowing yer living in t'same 'ouse as a murderer."

There followed a long silence. Pippa stared at Lucy enviously, wishing that *she'd* discovered the body. If she'd had those lines, she would have said them *much* more dramatically.

Eventually, Dr Rodgers spoke. "Mr Gough…I wonder if you would be good enough to ring the police. And…I must ask…insist…that none of you leave this house."

Chapter Ten

Miss Maud's body had been removed. As the death was unexpected there was to be an autopsy. The police surgeon had taken over, releasing Dr Rodgers from his duties. Dr Rodgers, recovered from his initial irritation at being called out so early in the morning, had arranged for his junior partner to take morning surgery and was now firmly ensconced in the deep, comfortable chair he had professed to despise. The logs on the fire were burning merrily as he sipped a fourth glass of port, his eyes were gradually closing, his breathing becoming deeper and deeper until it developed into such a sonorous snorting that Alicia jumped out of her chair.

"James. I cannot stay here a minute longer. I'll go mad if I have to listen to that disgusting noise."

"Perhaps we could go for a walk," ventured Pippa tentatively.

"Well…" began James doubtfully.

"Well nothing." Alicia stood up resolutely. "Come on Pippa. There's no earthly reason why we shouldn't go out. There's no-one here to stop us anyway."

"Hang on." Maggie rose from the settee. "I'll come too."

"Wait for me." Lucy who'd been sitting quietly by her mother's side, leapt to her feet.

Cook, to whom protocol was second nature, grabbed her arm, and whispered urgently, "You watch yersen, young 'un. 'Taint your place to go wi'them. An' anyway, we'd better get some cooking done if folks 'as to stay." Lucy returned to her seat sulkily and Fran, feeing sorry for the girl, patted her arm.

"You're an important witness, dear. The police will want to talk to you as soon as they arrive. Oh dear. What a dreadful business this is. They can't *really* think Maud was murdered, can they?" She looked around her, questioningly. "I mean, who would do such a thing? There's only us here." Leo, having exceeded the doctor's consumption of port, remained silent, sinking deeper and deeper into the chair, his tiny eyes almost disappearing and his cheeks approaching the same colour as the port.

Tom, nervously biting his fingernails, shook his head. "I don't know what to think Fran. I know I wish Maggie and I hadn't come here."

"What do *you* think, Harry?"

Fran turned to her husband, but Harry was too busy looking out of the window to answer his wife's question. The three young women were walking down the drive, battling against the elements and in obviously animated conversation. Harry smiled as he watched their progress, hypnotised by Pippa's slender young swaying hips, provocatively poured into a pair of skin-tight red jeans.

Fran turned to look at Aggie, standing straight-backed behind a chair, her normally darting eyes stilled, staring straight ahead into seeming oblivion. Cook, following Fran's gaze, shook her head.

"She's still in shock," she whispered. "I think she awt to lay down for a bit."

Aggie shook her head, fiercely. "Ah can 'ear yer. Ah'll stay 'ere."

"Then sit down," suggested Fran, kindly.

But Aggie shook her head again. "Am OK. Just…leave me be."

"I dun't see why I couldn't 'ave gone with 'em, Mam. *I'm* fed up staying in an' all. An' I've had a big shock. An' I live 'ere. They dun't. Am just as entitled as them ter go out. More entitled." Lucy's voice grew louder and louder as she gradually moved away from her mother.

"Don't start, Lucy. I can't be doin' wi' yer claptrap just now." Cook's voice rose warningly and Lucy, recognizing the danger, moved completely out of reach before continuing.

"Am just as good as them," she shouted. "An' am sick of skivvyin' for' em."

"Eee, I'm real sorry. Mr Leo. I'll tek er out."

"She's upset, Cook," said Fran gently. "Bound to be. She'll be alright, don't you fret."

"Here's a police car."

Harry stood and then sat down quickly, recalling Leo's insistence that 'he was in charge now'. He had no intention of being insulted again. But Leo was fast asleep, snoring alternatively, in competition with and slightly ahead of Dr Rodgers.

Harry sighed and rose to his feet again. Someone had to deal with the police and he was, after all, still the Hepplewhite's legal representative. "Try to waken those two will you Tom please?"

Harry spoke with what he considered to be justified self-righteousness as he viewed Dr Rodgers. He would *never* drink on duty, he told himself, conveniently forgetting how aggrieved he'd felt at not being offered a glass of Maud's best port.

DC Brocklebank, in the area on a routine inquiry, had received a message to say that a police presence was urgently required at Bishop Grange. There was no indication as to the nature of the problem, but the young detective was certain it would be a burglary. He guessed there would be some good stuff in the old house and antiques were being stolen and disposed of with alarming regularity these days.

As he drove up the long drive, he passed the three young women, scarves tucked over their noses against the driving snow. Bringing the car to a halt with a screech, he jumped out of the vehicle and confronted the startled trio. These were the accomplices. He could feel it in his bones.

DC Brocklebank had complete faith in his intuition. Unfortunately, that faith was not shared by his colleagues. Neither was it reflected in his percentage of success. In fact, the general consensus in the force was that Brockers, as his peers called him, was as thick as pig shit in a bottle.

"Right...get in. No if or buts. Just get in."

"Who the hell are you?" demanded Maggie.

"Detective Constable Brocklebank," he replied importantly, flashing his identity card.

"We'd better do as he says, hadn't we?" giggled Pippa, touching his arm. "He feels so *strong.*"

Brockers pulled back sharply.

"Don't do that, Miss. Such an action could be construed as assaulting a police officer in the execution of his duty."

Alicia climbed elegantly into the back of the car. "Don't be so bloody stupid man. Your superiors will hear of this. You will drive us back to the house. *Now.*"

Pippa gazed at her admiringly. She wished she'd said that. She could have been really dramatic if only she'd thought of it first.

The detective followed the women in to the house, undaunted by what he considered Alicia's arrogance. He'd read all the Agatha Christie's and always watched 'The Bill' so he'd seen it all before. The protests of innocence. The indignation. The veneer, which he knew would wear off after a few hours of professional questioning. Oh yes. He knew how to get under the skin.

First play the tough cop. Follow that with a bit of sympathy. Add a few threats of custodial sentence. Smoke a cigarette. Send for coffee...for one. Drink slowly and with relish. Then, in for the kill. A promise that the judge would be told how helpful they had been and bingo. They'd be eating out of his hand.

Harry met them in the hall. "Cook's going to make some sandwiches, my dears. You must be freezing. Go back to the sitting room whilst I acquaint this policeman with the facts."

DC Brocklehurst watched with dismay as his suspects disappeared through the open door.

"You know them Mr Gough?" The two men had met many times in court.

"Certainly I do. They are...were...are...Miss Maud's house guests." Harry's command of the English language momentarily deserted him, and he wasn't quite sure which tense to use now that their host was deceased.

"Has much been taken?" The detective quickly recovered his composure. A sure sign of a true copper, he always thought.

"Just the body," replied Harry vaguely, still feeling weak at the sight of Pippa's hypnotic hips. "Pull yourself together man," he remonstrated with himself sharply. He'd helped prosecute many a man for doing physically what he was doing mentally at this moment.

"Valuable, was it? The body. Ancient mummy or something?" He tapped the side of his nose. "Like...something from Egypt that...well...shouldn't be here." Brockers had been watching programs on Egyptology and considered himself a bit of an expert on the subject. This could be a case right up his street.

Harry stared at him, once more in full control of his senses. Ah, yes. The idiot bobby. He recognized him now. Why on *earth* had he been sent out to a case as important as this?

"What do you mean, boy...valuable?" he asked testily "What on earth do you think you're here for?"

"The burglary sir."

"It's a *murder*, you stupid man. Miss Maud Hepplewhite is dead. Murdered. And I think I know who perpetrated the crime."

Chapter Eleven

"Is everyone here who was present at the time the killing took place?" DC Brocklebank took out his pocket book and meticulously wrote the date at the top of the page. He had on several occasions been in trouble for altering dates and he was determined that there would be no technical faux pas on *this* case. This case was going to be his piece de resistance. His hour of triumph. This was the case that was going to elevate him to sergeant.

"Excuse me Constable," sighed Harry. "Is...anyone else coming? I mean...are you in charge of the inquiry? Surely one of your superiors should be in attendance."

Brockers drew himself up to his full height. "I trust...Mr Gough... you are not casting aspersions on my ability to conduct this affair satisfactorily."

"Well," replied Harry dryly, "it has to be said that your question was entirely inappropriate. It has not yet been established when the killing actually took place."

Leo, fully awake now, stood and pointed at Lucy. *"And,"* he roared belligerently, "we don't even know if this stupid bitch is lying. We only have her word that the cushion *was* on Maud's face."

Lucy's face crumbled. "It were. It were that cushion Miss Maud 'ad in 'er wheelchair. I'm not a liar, am I Mam? Mam, whar if t'murderer does me in?" She began to cry noisily. "Mam...I'm feart."

"Come come now, girl," Harry tut-tutted. Don't be silly." He took off his glasses and thoughtfully tapped his teeth with the stem. "Constable...at the risk of incurring your wrath..."

He paused dramatically. Pippa giggled appreciatively and Harry rewarded her with a slight movement of his thin lips, indicating he was aware of her support. "I think I will ask Inspector Locky to..."

"What the hell are *you* doing here, Brocklebank?"

The door burst open and Harry breathed a sigh of relief as the doorway was filled with six foot six of supreme police authority...in plain clothes.

"Ah, Thomas. Thank goodness. And Sergeant McTavish too."

A man of smaller build but with the same air of confidence as his superior had followed Inspector Locky into the room.

"Sirs." DC Brocklebank almost saluted. "I...picked up a message on my radio. It sounded urgent. Thought I'd better get here quick as possible sir."

"Well…now you're here you'd better stay. Might learn a thing or two." From the tone of Inspector Locky's voice, it was obvious that in his opinion, the prospect of Brockers ever learning anything to do with policing was as remote as the proverbial pig sprouting wings and taking to the sky.

"Right." The inspector took out his notebook and licked the end of a pencil. "Is everyone here who was…" he paused and looked around the room. Brockers flashed a triumphant glance at Harry. "Is everyone here who was on the premises between the time Miss Maud retired for the night and the time she was discovered deceased?"

"I…think I can answer that, Thomas." Harry felt he could now 'pull rank' on Leo. Leo might be the new owner of Bishop Grange, although Harry had his own thoughts on that, which he intended to relay to the inspector later. However, this was an official matter which he, Harry, was at ease with. "There are eight of us here as Miss Maud's guests, although it was to have been a working weekend for just four of us. Leo, Miss Maud's cousin, Miss Maggie McCriel, architect, James Brent, building consultant and myself, the Hepplewhite's legal representative. Aggie, you know, of course. Cook and her daughter, Lucy. I think I can say with impunity that…yes…we were all in the house from the time Miss Maud retired until the body was discovered by Lucy."

"That's not quite true," interrupted James. "If you remember Harry, when I returned from seeing my wife, who'd gone to bed early, both Leo and Pippa were outside. You said words to the effect that Pippa had taken him outside to cool him down."

"Clear his head," murmured Harry thoughtfully. "Yes, of course. Thank you, James."

"And why would he need to clear his head?" The inspector turned to Leo. "Had you been drinking, sir?"

There was an uncomfortable silence in the room as each person recalled Leo's behaviour the previous night.

"Come now. I need to know exactly where everyone was. And why."

"May I speak?" All eyes turned to Pippa, who was now standing, winding a blonde curl around her fingers.

"Sit down," muttered Leo. "You'll only make a fool of yourself…as usual." Harry, recognizing the hurt hiding behind Pippa's bright smile and nervous giggle as Leo's biting remark registered, had a glorious vision of personally genitally mutilating him.

"I think, sir, I'll be the judge of that." Inspector Locky turned to Pippa. "And you, madam, are…?"

Pippa's lips trembled as she attempted a sweet smile and Harry's blood pounded in his veins. He felt a surge of jealousy, an emotion so unfamiliar to him he was totally confused for a few seconds. Then, in a blinding, revealing flash, his feelings became crystal clear. He was in love with this girl. He didn't want her to smile like that at anyone else. He was overcome with emotion, dizzy with desire and he staggered, almost falling over. James grabbed his arm and helped him to a chair.

"Are you OK. Harry? Can I get you a drink?" James moved towards the drinks cabinet.

"No..no. I'm perfectly alright, thank you James."

Harry quickly recovered his composure…and his equilibrium.

Fran, after two attempts, rocking like a nodding dog in the back of a car, rose from the depths of the chair and began to fuss around him.

"Leave me alone, Fran," he said tetchily. "It's…nothing."

"It's his age," she nodded confidentially, to no one in particular. "He's been having problems. Do you know, I think men suffer from the menopause too. Do you think doctor, that could be the cause of…well…you know…men's little difficulties?"

Tom remained silent and Dr Rodgers was in too much of an alcoholically induced state of euphoria to even hazard a guess as to the cause of Harry's 'little difficulties'.

"Don't tell me Gough, you've got a touch of the old brewer's droop." Leo laughed gleefully. "Not my problem, eh Pippa?"

"Don't be coarse, Leo," replied Pippa primly.

Lucy looked puzzled. "Mam…what's…"

Cook spoke firmly to her daughter. "*Don't* ask, girl."

The inspector coughed and turned his attention to Pippa.

"My dear." He smiled and spoke gently. He too, a wise and hardened old cynic, suddenly felt protective towards her. "Would you like to speak to us in private? In fact," he added hastily, "if *anyone* wants to speak to us in private, please do so."

"No…no. I only wanted to say…yes, Leo had a little too much to drink. But…he often does. And he got a bit…well…rough. So…I took him outside. For a little walk. We didn't stay out long. It was ever so cold. So we came in and went to bed."

"And you are...Leo's wife?"

"No," giggled Pippa. "I'm his...partner."

"I see. And you were with him all night?"

"Course she was," interrupted Leo vehemently. "Where the hell do you think she was? Hopping from bed to bed like a bloody flea?"

"And neither of you ever left the bedroom?" persisted the inspector.

Pippa opened her mouth to speak, but Leo surreptitiously squeezed her arm, an action that did not pass unnoticed by Harry and she remained silent.

Harry rose to his feet. "Perhaps Thomas, we could have a word." He looked around the room. "I think you should all be prepared to stay here another night. Except you, of course, Doctor Rodgers."

The doctor, on hearing his name, opened his eyes and realizing his glass was empty, held it out to Harry.

"Don't mind if I do Gough, thanks. Cracking good port."

Harry released the glass from Dr Rodger's determined grasp.

"You have your surgery to attend this evening," he said firmly. "I think perhaps I'll send for a taxi to take you home. But for the rest, the weather is deteriorating anyway so it would be foolish to drive any distance in these inclement conditions. Aggie, perhaps you will arrange that please. And I'm sure Cook will be able to...er...rustle up some...er...suitable nourishment for all of us."

He glanced at Leo, expecting some remark about this being his house now and what did he think he was doing, inviting people to stay. But Leo's expression was impassive and he remained silent.

Harry, deliberately avoiding looking at Pippa, turned to the inspector. "Thomas, let us adjourn to the library."

James rose quickly to his feet. He'd been battling with his principles, which had been instilled into him by constant brainwashing at his public school, that one didn't snitch on one's fellow man...or woman.

"I too, would like to speak to you, Inspector. In private, please."

Pippa giggled nervously. "Well...in that case...I think I'd like to speak to you again, Inspector."

"In private?" asked the inspector, raising his eyebrows.

Pippa stood up, smoothing her already smooth jeans over slender hips and walked across the room to sit beside Fran.

"Yes, please." She nodded vigorously. "In private."

"Right, now we're getting somewhere. Inspector Locky rubbed his hands together in satisfaction. But first, I'll speak to the girl...Lucy."

"Aaaah." Lucy began to wail.

Harry turned to Cook and whispered, "You'd better go with her."

"Sergeant McTavish."

"Sir." The sergeant sprang to attention, ready to do his master's bidding.

"You come with me. Brocklebank, you stay here. No-one is to leave this room. And Brockers..."

"Sir." DC Brocklebank took a deep breath, eager to take part in the proceedings.

"For God's sake...just keep your mouth shut."

Chapter Twelve

"Lucy...you're a bright girl. You do realize what you're saying, don't you?"

"She's tellin' truth Mr Locky."

"Please Lily. Let your daughter speak for herself."

Cook's face flushed, not because of the inspector's gentle rebuke, but because he had called her by her Christian name. It was so seldom anyone called her anything other than Cook, she sometimes wondered if she had an identity.

She'd never forgotten her feeling of despair and total humiliation the day she'd sought an audience with the mistress of the country house she'd worked in, to confess that she was pregnant. The daughter of the house...a mere lass of thirteen and whom Cook had known since the day she was born...had looked her up and down with a knowing look and an insolent sneer. "Mummy," she'd called. "That...*person*...from the kitchen wants to speak to you."

Lily Turner and Thomas Locky had attended the same school and had been in the same class for a year. Although he was a couple of years younger than her, because he was a clever lad he'd been put in a class ahead. And Lily, because she had been a trifle slow with her reading, had been held back for a year.

She'd been a bonny lass in those days and Tom-Tom...so nick-named because he claimed he could do it twice in quick succession...had once kissed her. Tom said that if the head prefect hadn't poked his head round the bike shed unexpectedly, he fancied her so much his name would have changed to Tom-Triple-Tom.

Lily sighed. All so long ago. All such silly, school boy stuff. And of course, he would have forgotten. Thomas had got on in life, as everyone knew he would. Didn't even speak with a Yorkshire accent anymore. But...it was good that he had at least remembered her name.

"Go on, Lucy. You tell t'inspector anything you can. 'Ee wont let anybody 'urt yer."

"Sergeant, take notes. Now Lucy. I want you to tell me, in your own words, *exactly* what you saw when you went into Miss Maud's room. And *exactly* what time it was."

Cook was mistaken. Thomas had not forgotten their tryst behind the bike shed. His eyes watered even now as he recalled the kisses they had exchanged. She'd been like a little dumpling in his arms. Ah well. All so long ago. All such silly, schoolboy stuff.

"Your Mum's right. Lucy," he said gently. "No one's going to hurt you. Just so long as you tell the truth."

....

Harry Gough handed Inspector Locky a Havana. Although Miss Maud hadn't smoked herself, she'd always kept a good supply of quality cigars for visitors and he felt obliged to offer hospitality on his deceased client's behalf.

"It's a rum do this, Harry."

Inspector Thomas Locky and Harry were old acquaintances, both professionally and socially, having bared their breasts and rolled up a trouser leg when being initiated into the mystics of their Masonic Lodge. They'd played a twosome on the golf course occasionally and met frequently in the nineteenth.

"Can you throw any light on it? Unofficially, of course."

Sergeant Jock McTavish had been dispatched back into the sitting room to keep an eye on Brockers, who had a reputation for jumping to conclusions without any evidence and the inspector had often found himself having to smooth many jangled nerves.

Harry removed his spectacles and gave them an unnecessary polish.

"If Miss Maud had not...died...when she did, Leo Hepplewhite would have been written out of her will. And...she informed him of her decision last evening in front of everyone, just before she retired. As far as I am aware, no one else here has any reason to want her dead. And as there seems to be no question of it being an outside job...need I say more?"

"Mmm. So you're saying Harry, he had ample opportunity to slip into her bedroom, place the cushion over her and suffocate her. He's a big fellow. She wouldn't have been able to struggle even. That would mean that the Pippa girl is in cahoots with him. She says he never left the bedroom."

With a sinking heart, Harry realized that if Leo had killed his cousin, Pippa may indeed be involved.

"Where's the cushion?" continued the inspector. "We'll need it for forensic. It'll be sad if the girl's implicated. Bonny little thing." He sighed. "I must be getting old, Harry. Starting to feel sorry for a pretty face."

"The cushion? Never thought about it. I suppose it's still in Miss Maud's bedroom."

"Right. Let's have it out then."

The inspector strode purposefully across the room, opened the door and shouted. "Brockers. Come."

"Yes Sir. Here, Sir."

"Go upstairs and bring…what's it like, Harry?"

"I think…yes…it's black. Black velvet. That is if Lucy's observations are correct. If it is the one from the wheelchair."

"Find Miss Maud's bedroom, lad. There should be a black velvet cushion in there. Bring it down here. No…wait. Go fetch some gloves and a plastic bag from the car. Handle it carefully. Forensics'll go berserk if we mess it up. Before you go, ask Mr….er," he glanced at his notes, "Mr Brent to come in. You'd best leave us Harry. Ask McTavish to come back, if you would."

……………………

"You've travelled a long way, Mr Brent," began the inspector pleasantly. "What do you think to Yorkshire? Do, please sit down. Not that you will have seen much of it, I don't suppose."

"My father was born in Yorkshire, Inspector. And I have relatives in the area. Not that I've seen much of them recently, although I visited Yorkshire quite a lot in my early days."

"And your wife?"

"It's her first visit." James had no intention of repeating Alicia's derogatory remarks about Yorkshire. He knew from experience that Yorkshire folk did not take kindly to criticism of their county.

"Right." Anyone who knew Inspector Locky was aware that when this word was spoken, it meant that the niceties were over, the interview had begun and it was time to get down to business.

"What do you want to tell me, Mr Brent?"

James hesitated. "Well, I don't *really* know where to begin."

The inspector leaned back in his chair. He remained silent, his face impassive.

"It's…the McCriels. Tom and Maggie. I mean Tom. Well, both of them, I suppose."

James stared at the inspector for inspiration but the officer's face was expressionless.

"Last night...early evening really, 'cos Alicia went to bed as soon as she'd helped Miss Maud into bed, I saw Tom coming out of Maud's bedroom. She'd asked him...well no, she'd *told* him she wanted to speak to him and to go to her room."

James paused, still unsure of whether to repeat the conversation he'd over-heard. There was a long silence.

Eventually, the inspector spoke. "Mr Brent, this is a possible *murder* inquiry, you understand."

"Yes. Yes, I do understand, Inspector. OK. I heard Miss Maud threaten him."

"Threaten?"

"Yes. She said she would have him struck off. You know. Off the register. He's a doctor, you see."

"And why would she say that?" asked the inspector, blandly.

James looked down at his shoes. He couldn't bring himself to say why, although he had a pretty good idea.

"I don't know, Inspector." James lifted his head and met his questioner's eyes unflinchingly. "I don't know," he repeated firmly. He felt he'd set the ball rolling. Let someone else dish the dirt if they wanted to.

Both men sat in silence, both tense, the officer willing him to say more. James lips remained closed and the officer relaxed.

"Alright, Mr Brent. Did Tom...Mr McCriel reply?"

"Yes. He turned back into the bedroom. He was there for quite a while. I...couldn't hear anything. Then he came out, saying something like 'I'll take a note of that'. I can't remember his exact words. He saw me. He looked a bit embarrassed. After that he went into his room. I didn't see him until the following...well...this morning. It seems such a long time ago."

"Did you hear Miss Maud say anything else?"

"It's not there, sir."

"Constable Brocklebank. How many times do I have to tell you? Do not barge into a room when I'm interviewing someone. I do apologize, Mr Brent. You were saying...?"

James stood up, grateful for the interruption. "That's OK. I've...nothing more to say."

"You're sure about that?"

"Yes," replied James firmly.

"Mm. Right, Brockers. Let's find this cushion."

"Lucy, when you took the cushion off Miss Maud's face, what did you do with it?"

Lucy stared at the inspector blankly. He tried again. "Lucy, have you got Miss Maud's cushion?"

Lucy shuddered. "No. What would I want wi' that. I left it weer it were."

"Thank you Lucy. You can go now."

DC Brocklebank turned to his superior eagerly. "That means then sir, whoever's taken the cushion must be the murderer."

"Can I come in, please?"

Pippa smiled at Lucy as she left the room. "Inspector, James says that you're looking for Miss Maud's cushion."

He nodded. "That's right, Miss."

"Well...I've got it."

DC Brocklebank stepped forward. "Shall I caution her sir, or will you?"

Chapter Thirteen

"You see Inspector," began Pippa earnestly, her bright blue eyes opening wide as she spoke. "Little Lucy was in a *terrible* state and quite frankly, I was petrified. It reminded me of a play I was in. I couldn't sleep for *weeks* after." Pippa warmed to her subject. "There was this old lady, not unlike Miss Maud, except Miss Maud isn't old...er...wasn't old. Which is it, Inspector, when someone's dead? Is it isn't or wasn't or ...well anyway, I was the maid you see and I...."

"It's not isn't...it's wasn't...oh shit. Look, could we *please* stick to the cushion? Sorry, Miss. I didn't mean to..." The inspector gave himself a shake. What the hell was he doing, apologizing to the girl?

Pippa stared at him blankly for a few seconds. "Oh yes. Well you see, I must have taken it from Lucy. She was crying so hard. It was heartbreaking. That's why I left her in Fran's...Mrs Gough's care. I didn't even realize I was holding it until Leo mentioned it."

"Tell me Miss...er...Pippa. Was your...was Leo awake when you went back in the bedroom?"

"No, he was still asleep. I had to shake him really hard to wake him."

"Perhaps he hadn't slept much," suggested the inspector.

"Well if he hadn't, it was nothing to do with me. There was no sex. Because you see, Inspector..."

"Please...Miss," interrupted Locky. "I'm not interested in your...in Mr Hepplewhite's sexual activities. I was merely wondering if he had something on his mind. Was he worrying about anything."

He paused, waiting for Pippa to respond, but again she gazed at him blankly. "So, what did Leo say when he saw you with the cushion?" he prompted.

Pippa's brow wrinkled, like a child struggling with its homework. "Oh dear. I can't remember the exact words. It was all so...up*setting*. Does it matter, Inspector?"

"Trouble is, you may have inadvertently destroyed some forensic evidence."

"What do you mean?"

"Well, there may have been saliva and other substances on the cushion which would substantiate that the cushion was actually on Maud's face. And also particles of skin."

"Oh Inspector. I'm so sorry. I didn't know." Pippa's eyes filled with tears and she began to cry.

"Now now, my dear," began the inspector.

Sergeant McTavish, who had now rejoined them, coughed discreetly. Locky recognized the warning sign from his faithful watchdog, reminding him that even the most beautiful and innocent looking women are capable of committing the most heinous of crimes.

"Right, young lady." Locky resumed his authoritative tone. "Did you have any ulterior motive in removing that cushion? Your boyfriend...Leo Hepplewhite, stands to gain a great deal from his cousin's death. In fact, it was rather fortuitous, wouldn't you say, that she died when she did. She had threatened to change her will, hadn't she?"

Pippa remained silent. Inspector Locky waited patiently. His years in the force had taught him that policing is very much a waiting game.

Sergeant McTavish stood erect by the door like a sentinel on duty. Although the two men had joined the force about the same time, McTavish had never begrudged Locky his superior position. He acknowledged that the big, burly officer was not merely brawn but was endowed with a quicksilver brain and a temperament entirely suited to investigative work. As the seconds ticked by, he recalled his first day in CID when he had kept watch during the night on a house of ill repute. Locky had been assigned to keep observations outside the front door. The door had opened unexpectedly and Locky had dropped quickly to the ground. It was pitch black. As he lay there, a man had unfastened his zip and urinated. Locky had taken the full stream on his face without a movement and was promoted to sergeant because of the success of the raid. From that day on, in McTavish's eyes, Locky could do no wrong.

Pippa sighed deeply. "That's been bothering me, Inspector. That's what I want to talk to you about. Leo said we were both in the bedroom all night. He was lying. He thought I was asleep. He got up ever so quietly and went out. I don't know how long he was out cos I *was* asleep when he came back. Well, I must have been cos I never heard him come back. But...I'm sure he wouldn't have done anything to hurt Miss Maud. I think he has plenty of money of his own."

"Can you remember what time he went out of the room?" asked Locky quietly.

"Yes. I looked at my watch. It was exactly midnight."

"That will be all, Pippa. Thank you for your co-operation. That has been most helpful."

Pippa hesitated. "Will you…do you…will Leo know what I've told you? He'll never forgive me if he finds out."

Sergeant McTavish gently propelled the girl out of the door. "Thank you, Miss."

Closing the door behind her, he waited till he was sure she was out of earshot.

"Does that leave her in the clear, do you reckon, Thomas?"

The inspector frowned. "It's pointing to Leo. But…musn't close our minds Jock. Remember the Ripper. And there's the young doctor. We need some tests doing on that blessed cushion. Trouble is, Leo could now say he handled it when Pippa brought it into the bedroom. Damn the girl."

"What about the doctor?"

"Tom McCriel. Let's have him in, Jock. Find out why Miss Maud threatened to have him struck off. I think James Brent knows more than he's prepared to say. Public school and all that, I should think. These bods close rank in times of adversity. Same with that Lucan chap. Old pal's act."

"Yes…but he did *tell* us of Miss Maud's threat, Thomas."

"Mmm. Get the feeling it was not so much public spiritedness as not wanting his wife to be the last person to see Miss Maud. Other than the murderer, if indeed it turns out to *be* murder. Look at the weather. There's a blizzard blowing out there. What's the time, Jock? Wonder if we should bed down for the night. Have you anything pressing to go home for?"

Jock McTavish laughed. "It's six o clock. Have a couple of old bachelors like us ever anything to rush home for?"

"Right. Let Brockers know. And Jock, send for a car to pick that cushion up. There'll be one somewhere in the vicinity. And find Aggie will you? She'll fix us up with beds. But before you do that, get that young doctor in here. McCriel."

"What about the sister? You know Thomas, I can hardly believe she's a qualified architect. She looks so young. They both do, don't you think?"

Locky smiled. "Haven't you noticed how young our new bobbies are looking, Jock? It's us, man. We're old. Getting past it."

"No…not you Thomas. Not you."

…………………………

81

Tom McCriel fingered his collar nervously. Inspector Locky continued writing his notes, completely ignoring the young man sitting opposite him. "You...wanted to see me?" Tom's voice faltered slightly.

Locky looked up from his writing as if surprised to see him there. He shrugged his shoulders. "Not really," he said, as if the thought had never occurred to him and he carried on writing.

Sergeant McTavish smiled to himself. He'd seen his boss in action before. "Keep them in suspense, Jock," he would say. "Get them on the defensive."

"In that case I'll..." Tom half rose to his feet.

"Sit down." The voice hit the unsuspecting young doctor like a whiplash and he dropped back into his chair with a swiftness that surprised even the inspector.

"This was going to be easy," he thought. "A Southern softie. I'll go straight for the jugular."

"Right. Miss Maud was going to have you struck off the medical register. Is that why you killed her?"

Locky returned to his writing, leaving Tom breathless and open-mouthed.

"I never...I didn't...Inspector, you're *wrong.*" Tom's voice rose to a high tenor.

The inspector threw his pen down on the table. "You're a killer, if ever I saw one. I know it. The sergeant here knows it, don't you Sarge? DC Brocklebank knew it as soon as he saw you. Up and coming young detective is Brockers. Has instinct. Uncanny. Never wrong."

Sergeant McTavish stifled a chuckle. "May God forgive you, Thomas," he thought.

The inspector pushed back his chair noisily and stood up, towering over the shrinking young man. "You're a monster. You killed a defenceless disabled woman. And you a doctor. Take over McTavish. I can't bear to look at this man any longer."

He stormed out of the room, leaving Tom ashen-faced and shaking.

"Phew. Never seen him like this before, Tom."

The sergeant turned round the chair his boss had vacated. Swinging his leg over the seat, he leaned with arms folded on the back and smiled at the quivering young doctor.

"Would you like a cuppa, lad?"

Tom shook his head.

"Ciggy?"

"No. I don't...thanks. Listen, I'd no idea you were thinking that I...I mean...I *couldn't*. I'm a doctor. I couldn't *kill.*"

"Some do," said McTavish mildly. "Crippen did. Why don't you tell me all about it? You'd never met Miss Maud before, had you? Why was she going to have you struck off? What had you done to make her threaten to do that?"

"Was it James who told you?" asked Tom dully. "I knew he'd heard."

"Tell me lad, before the inspector comes back."

Tom shook his head. "I can't, Sergeant. It involves some one else. I can't tell anyone."

Sergeant McTavish studied Tom's face carefully. It was twisted with anguish. "The inspector will find out eventually, son. He always does. Tell me," he cajoled.

Tom's lips tightened. He shook his head, like a schoolboy refusing to admit he'd been smoking.

"Suit yourself." The sergeant's voice hardened. "Then I can't do anything for you. We'd better join the others. Come on."

Aggie met them in the hall. "Beds are made up Sergeant McTavish. Two of yer will 'ave to share. An' Cook sez ter tell yer t'dinner'll be ready in ten minutes. Can I go ter bed?"

The sergeant hesitated. "Best not, Aggie. The inspector wants to check some times. You'll probably be able to help."

....

An air of gloom and despondency hung over the sitting room. The heavy curtains had been drawn. The room was warm enough, logs from the estate ensured that, but there was a chill in the air. There had been a death in the house. Not a natural departure. One of them could be responsible for that departure and, from time to time, they each surreptitiously viewed their neighbour with suspicion.

The old clock in its comfortable, undisputed position in the corner still ticked, the pendulum still swung, but James, increasingly fanciful since arriving here, was sure he detected some sadness in its timeless movement. A requiem perhaps? Did it know that sooner rather than later, because of the turn of events, it would be whisked off to some saleroom? Heartlessly poked and prodded by uncaring fingers and then, vulnerable and no longer belonging, auctioned and whisked off to...where? Shipped off to America?

Tom and Maggie sat close together on a settee, Tom still pale and shaking. Inspector Locky was in close conversation with his sergeant, while DC Brocklebank walked up and down the room, his brow furrowed and hands behind his back as he'd seen his hero, Hercule Poirot do. Alicia was playing patience with a totally disinterested expression on her face. James, tiring of his pointless thoughts tried to engage her, to no avail, in conversation. Leo had opened another bottle of port which he was disinclined to share with anyone. Fran and Pippa were deep in conversation whilst Harry's eyes devoured Pippa's pretty face with a hunger he knew he should be hiding.

The door opened and Cook popped her head round the door.

"Dinner's ready." She glanced at Thomas Locky for his approval and when it came in the form of a nod and a suggestion of a smile, she burst into tears.

"Oh *Christ,*" exploded Leo, spilling the port on to the carpet. "Why am I surrounded by stupid women?"

All eyes focused, as if hypnotised, on the deep blood-red stain spreading in all directions and then slowly disappearing into the heavily patterned carpet.

Pippa shivered as she recalled touching that dead cheek, the dullness of Maud's eyes, the smell of death that had filled her nostrils. An uneasy silence stretched out interminably. No one sprang forward to mop up the spillage. It was unimportant.

Anxious for some diversion, Harry unnecessarily cleared his throat. "Let's not keep Cook waiting."

Led by Fran, always ready for replenishment under any circumstances, they walked slowly and silently in single file across the hall and into the dining room, looking incongruously like a school crocodile. DC Brocklebank brought up the rear as if in anticipation of one of them leaping out and escaping. He stopped at the dining room door to write in his notebook. 'A lugubrious procession proceeded into the dining room.' Closing the book with a satisfied flourish, he promised himself he would remember that sentence for his memoirs.

Chapter Fourteen

Dinner was a sombre affair, although the three policemen ate heartily. DC Brocklebank's analysis of this ability to place events in separate boxes in the mind was that a policeman is a special breed. One of a chosen few. It allowed them to stand back and review a situation clinically and unemotionally, allowing them to live a near normal life. His two superiors didn't need to analyse why they were able to partake so readily of Cook's superb offering. They were merely hungry, the aromas drifting across the hall reminding them that it was a long time since breakfast.

"Shame to waste it."

Fran, whose appetite was stimulated by any emotion, tucked enthusiastically into her third helping of pudding after the other women had refused to have any at all.

Harry had been watching Pippa toying daintily with her food and followed suit, in an effort to identify with her. Cook stayed in the kitchen and the meal was served, albeit reluctantly, by a tight-lipped Aggie and a fearful Lucy, who unnerved some and irritated others with her constant, frightened glances around as if expecting someone or something to leap out at her.

"Right." Inspector Locky stood up, indicating that the meal was over. "Aggie, can we have coffee in the sitting room, please? Then we can get on with this investigation."

"No coffee for me, thank you Aggie," said Fran. "Wouldn't mind a cup of tea though."

"Anybody else want tea?" Aggie, without any apparent reason, suddenly sounded affable. "Mr Leo, would tha like a nice cuppa tea?"

"No," replied Leo ungraciously. "I'm off to bed. I'm knack…"

"I'm sorry, Mr Hepplewhite," interrupted the inspector, not looking the least bit apologetic. "I need everyone together now, please. Aggie, that includes you, Cook and Lucy."

"Tea, Mr Brent?"

"Coffee please, Aggie."

"And you, Miss Alice?"

The inspector sighed impatiently, unable to decide whether Aggie was being deliberately obstructive in delaying his enquiries or if she felt she had to play host in the absence of her mistress.

"Aggie," he said, with the slightest suggestion of irritation, "a selection of both will do. Now...*please*...can we get on?"

....

"Will you tell me, Mrs Brent, at what time did you take Miss Maud up to her room?"

"It would be about 7.30," replied James.

"Mr Brent," the inspector snapped. "I don't mean to be rude, sir, but is your wife not capable of answering herself?"

James shuffled his feet uncomfortably. "Yes. It's just that...she's not been well since we came here. I thought she might be a bit confused."

"James, do shut up. I can remember quite well." Alicia turned to face the inspector and spoke precisely and without expression. "We had tea in here yesterday afternoon. About 5.30. Then we chatted. Miss Maud discovered that Leo wasn't divorced, that he was living over the brush with Pippa, and said she was going to make a new will."

"You bitch," said Leo sullenly.

"I say Leo, steady on. My wife is merely giving a true account of what happened. Go on, darling," said James, taking hold of Alicia's hand.

"Carry on, Mrs Brent," said the inspector, ignoring both of the men.

"She...Miss Maud, asked me to help her into her stair-lift. I straightened her cushion..."

"Ah yes, the cushion," murmured the inspector. "Sorry madam. Do continue."

"It was about 7.30. I went upstairs, helped her into bed, said goodnight and went to my own room. I was tired and went straight to bed. I knew no more until I heard a lot of shouting the following...this morning." Alicia picked up a magazine and began to read, making it clear that as far as she was concerned, that was the end of the matter.

"Er...yes. Right." Inspector Locky knew that was all he was going to get from her. "Mr McCriel, you went to Miss Maud's room at...what time?"

Maggie patted her brother's hand. "Go on, Tom," she whispered encouragingly.

Tom smiled and nodded to his sister. "As Miss Maud was leaving the room with Alicia, she said she wanted to see me in about ten minutes. I saw her at 7.45. She was in bed. We talked...and then I left."

"And...she was alive when you left her?"

Maggie leapt to her feet. "That's enough, Inspector. How dare you accuse my brother?"

Ignoring Maggie, the inspector fixed Tom with an icy stare. "Well. Was she?"

Sergeant McTavish viewed his superior with dog-like devotion, admiring his implacable manner and DC Brocklebank made a mental note of how to behave under fire.

"Yes...of course she was alive."

"Mr McCriel...I put it to you, you had the opportunity to kill Miss Maud. And it would appear you also had a motive. Mr McCriel...why was Maud threatening you with being struck off the medical register?"

Lucy, sitting at the back of the room with her mother and Aggie, took a deep breath and opened her mouth to speak.

"Don't you dare," whispered her mother, covering the girl's mouth with a large, work-reddened hand. "You keep yer mouth shut. It's nowt ter do wi'you."

There was a long silence. Pippa, sitting close to the fire gasped and drew back as a fiercely burning log spat out a knot as if condemning the silence and urging progress. The silence continued, broken only by the soft tapping of Inspector Locky's pencil on his notebook.

Maggie looked askance at Tom and when he nodded, she began to speak, clearly and decisively.

"It all began...oh...such a long time ago. My father was in the force. The police force. He was a gentle soul really. Much too nice a man to be a policeman."

DC Brocklebank tensed himself for a withering response but both his superiors sent him a warning glance and he settled for a malevolent glare at Maggie.

"He was a sergeant. A uniformed sergeant. But while he was escorting a prisoner to the court, the prisoner escaped and later killed someone. Dad was demoted. He was devastated. Spent the rest of his time in the office. And he hated it. He'd had high hopes of carving out a career in the CID. He had to stand by and watch young men, who'd joined later than him, doing well. Being promoted. He was a wonderful father. I can remember him being so kind to Tom and me. But he changed. Became dictatorial. He made all the decisions in the house. My mother couldn't even say what we would have to eat. He told me what to wear. And we stopped going out on the little trips like we used to. I was never allowed to bring any friends home and he wouldn't let me visit any of my school friends. Outside though, to others, he was just the same. Loving. Caring. And he was. Only…" she stopped.

Inspector Locky spoke softly to her, his experience telling him what was about to emerge.

"Miss McCriel…Maggie…would you like to continue this in private?" Maggie shook her head. "No. No, it's OK. It's a relief to speak out. Perhaps this is what was needed to make Tom and me admit to ourselves we do need help. One night…I think I would be about five years old. I'd just started school. I'd been asleep. I woke up as Dad carried me into his bed. His and Mum's bed. I lay between them and he…fondled me. I thought it was all right. Because he was my Dad, you see. After that, nearly every night,Mum would tell me to go and 'warm the bed for Daddy'. She started to stay in my bed on those nights."

"You poor child," whispered Fran.

When I was about ten or eleven, he began to have full sex with me."

"Dirty bastard," muttered Leo.

"Hush, Leo. Let Maggie speak."

Maggie flashed Pippa a grateful glance. "I tried to tell my teacher because he was hurting me but the teacher said I was wicked to make up stories like that. She said my daddy would go to prison if I told lies. I couldn't speak to my mother at all. She used to say, 'Daddy knows best. Daddy won't hurt you.' Tom was at boarding school by this time so I had no one. Then one day during the summer holidays Tom told me that Dad had been interfering with him too. He was sixteen. I was fourteen. One day, while Mum and Dad were out, we packed a case and caught a train to Blackpool. We'd an aunt there. She ran a bed and breakfast place. We told her what had been happening and fortunately she believed us. She wanted us to go to the police but we couldn't and she understood. He loved us, you see. And…in a strange sort of way…we still loved him too. And it would have killed our Mum if he'd have gone to prison. So…we just never went back."

She began to cry and the inspector and sergeant exchanged glances.

"Tell me, Maggie," asked the sergeant quietly, "what's this got to do with Miss Maud?"

Tom placed his fingers on his sister's lips. "I'll tell them, Maggie. We stayed with our aunt. Our mother used to write to us but we didn't reply and eventually the letters ceased. No birthday cards. No Christmas cards. Nothing. And…I think we were both glad. We went to university. The same one. Took a flat together. Just the two of us. We found it impossible, both of us, to have a relationship with anyone. Except…with each other." Tom paused for a while, then continued, passionately. "We loved one another, Inspector. We tried not to. We knew it was wrong but we couldn't help it." There followed a long silence. DC Brocklebank sidled to his boss's side.

"A word, sir," he whispered.

"What *is* it?" asked the inspector, testily.

"Incest sir. That's what it is. Shall I caution them or will you?"

"Piss off, Brockers. Carry on Mr McCriel."

"When we arrived here, we kissed as we walked towards the house. There was a movement at the window. I looked up and saw Miss Maud. I knew she'd seen us and would realize that…well…it was more than a brother and sister kiss."

"Yer see," whispered Lucy triumphantly to her mother. "I telt yer. Aggie 'eard 'em an' all. An' you *hit* me, Aggie. An' it 'urt."

Aggie stared straight ahead, an inscrutable expression on her lined, grey face. Inspector Locky watched her with interest. The last time he had seen her was when, as a raw recruit, he'd been sent with a sergeant to Bishop Grange. Miss Maud's mother…what was her name, he mused. Ah yes. Sarah. Sarah Hepplewhite. There'd been an accident. Her wheelchair had toppled down the stairs. She was dead when the police and doctor arrived. He could visualize Aggie now standing at the top of the stairs, stiff as a ramrod, her tiny black eyes darting everywhere. Alert. As she was now. And silent. That was…Locky did a quick calculation…must be thirty odd years ago. Probably more. And she'd already been in the Hepplewhite's service for over twenty years then. So she was in her seventies. Tough old bird. And from the look of her weighed hardly anything. And what did the old woman know? What lay behind those tiny black eyes? Perhaps there was nothing. Perhaps years of servile duty had dulled her senses, brain-washed her into the submissive caring of only the Hepplewhite family, without any thought of her own life. Or did there lay buried in that small head some dark secrets. She had lived here a lifetime. Longer than some of the Hepplewhites themselves. Did she have knowledge which her status insisted she musn't disclose?

Their eyes met and as hers flickered ever so slightly, he knew there were doors to be unlocked. But how? Aggie was one of the old school. How could he break down that role of 'upstairs downstairs' that Aggie had grown up with. That servants were as nothing in the eyes of their betters. And that they never spoke in condemnation of their masters.

Aggie would know everything that went on in this household. He was sure that she would have been aware of the McCriel's relationship. That she would have felt it her duty to tell her mistress. He knew that was where her loyalty would lie. He also knew that she would never divulge any information to an outsider. Certainly not to him.

....

At nine that evening the cushion had been collected by a reluctant young patrol driver with instructions to 'get his arse back to the station shit-hot'. The blizzard was increasing. Aggie had lit a fire in the library and the three officers sat huddled around it.

"Christ knows why anyone wants to live in a place like this," grumbled Sergeant McTavish. "It's bloody *perishing*."

"Yes," agreed Inspector Locky. "I should have asked Aggie to light it sooner. She's a poor looking soul isn't she? Wonder what will happen to her. And to Lily."

"Lily?" asked the sergeant, with a quirk of one eyebrow.

"Cook to you, Jock."

"Do you know her, Thomas?"

Locky smiled a secret smile. "I very nearly knew her a lot better," he laughed. "A long time ago."

"Maybe Harry will give us some details of the will." McTavish moved a little closer to the fire. "The cousin, Leo, says he's the sole beneficiary but surely some provision will have been made for the staff, don't you think Thomas?"

Thomas pursed his lips, drawing in a deep breath. "Wouldn't like to bet on it. Strange folk, these old families. Like to keep the money in the family."

"Well, in that case, if she hadn't met such an untimely end, who do you think she'd have left it to? She said she was going to cut Leo out."

"Ah...but would she have actually done it? We'll never know. However, Leo obviously thought she would cos it seems he was in a right mood last night. Nearly belted that girl of his. But she packs a real punch apparently. She's not the bit of Dresden China she appears to be. Been around a bit that one."

"So, who do you think killed her, sir?" DC Brocklebank asked excitedly.

"If you ask me, that Tom's our man."

"Well, no one asked you, Constable," replied Locky, putting the eager young man firmly in his place. "And what's more, let's have less talk of arrests and cautions from you. Just sit quiet and *listen*."

"But…what about the brother and sister? We can't turn a blind eye on that, sir. I shall, of course, submit my report in the usual way."

McTavish flinched. Locky gathered his breath ready for the onslaught. The verbal attack which followed left DC Brocklebank in no doubt what his parentage was, what the extent of his intelligence was, what his prospects for the future were and also what his prospects of ever becoming a father were if he dared to put on paper anything he'd heard during these investigations. He was also made aware that Inspector Locky, and Inspector Locky alone, was in charge of this case and that no snotty-nosed, wet behind the ears, incompetent constable had any opinions whatsoever that were worth listening to.

This was the first time the constable had crossed swords with his inspector and, totally shell-shocked, he knew now why even experienced coppers spoke in hushed tones whenever they mentioned 'big Tom's' name.

The attack was over as quickly as it had begun. Inspector Locky did not bear grudges. Well…not once he had totally demoralised his adversary and established his supreme authority.

"Fancy a beer you two?" he asked pleasantly, changing tack with consummate ease. "I understand Cook has a spanking brew tucked away in her kitchen. See to that Allen, will you please?"

DC Allan Brocklebank beamed his pleasure at being addressed by his first name. He couldn't wait to get back to the station to announce that he and Thomas were as close as two peas in a pod. He almost bowed as he backed out of the room.

When the mollified constable had disappeared, the inspector said quietly. "Look Jock, I don't want to make anything of this incest business. We're here on a murder inquiry. I'll have a word with those two. Make sure they take steps to sort themselves out. And tomorrow I reckon we'll be taking Leo Hepplewhite in. And Jock…don't tell Brockers or we'll probably find the bird has flown."

Chapter Fifteen

"*Right* James, when are we going to get down to some details on this housing thing?"

James stared at Leo in amazement. Did this man not realize he could be under suspicion of murder? He was impossible. His lack of sensitivity filled James with dismay. Amidst the sick example of human failings that were beginning to unfold, all the man could think of was making a killing. James stopped himself short, filled with horror at the thought that Leo could indeed be responsible for Maud's death.

"I refuse to discuss the matter Leo."

Unperturbed, Leo rose to his feet and yawned. "Might as well go to bed then. Come on Pippa."

"No, not yet. I'm not tired."

"I wasn't suggesting that you were," Leo smirked.

Harry felt a pain in his heart, like an icy dagger piercing his chest. The thought of Pippa making love with Leo disturbed him so much he felt ill. He gazed at her longingly, yearning to tell her how much he loved her.

"We might as well go too Harry." Fran struggled to her feet. "I don't suppose the inspector has any more to say tonight. Oh…I'm sure it's all a dreadful mistake. I mean…no-one here could *possibly* do such a wicked thing."

She waddled across the room to where Maggie and Tom were sitting. "I'm so sorry, my dears. But I'm sure it will all come right in the end. I'll just slip into the kitchen, Harry. See if Cook's left any tit-bits out. I can't understand why I'm so hungry. Most unusual."

Pippa looked serious. She hadn't been giggling very much lately.

"Leo, shouldn't you wait until the inspector comes back in before you go to bed?"

"Look…I'm not staying up half the night while those three idiots play cops and robbers."

"Well, you go, Leo. I'll stay here for a while."

"Suit yourself." Leo walked unsteadily to the door, almost falling over Lucy. "And *you*." He struggled for words as the girl shrank before him. "Don't ding that bleeding gong in the morning."

Cook took hold of her daughter's arm. "Cum on Lucy, love. It's time we were in bed 'an all. *We*…have an early start in t'morning. Cum on Aggie.

You've 'ad a bad day 'an all."

Alicia yawned. "I think I'll go too, James. I'll take a magazine and read, I think."

"Wait for me, Alicia."

James rose to his feet. He'd have a word with the inspector first thing in the morning. There really was no reason why he and Alicia should have to stay and, weather permitting, if they made an early start they could be home by midday.

Harry said nothing. He was hoping that Pippa would stay behind for a little while. He just wanted to be with her. No ulterior motive. Just to feast his eyes on her lovely face. And...to delay going to bed until Fran was asleep.

One by one they went upstairs, leaving Pippa and Harry alone. Harry knew that Fran would not return. She would have filled a dish with whatever food she could find to take to bed with her. Pippa sat in front of the dying embers of the log fire, stretching her bare toes towards the comfort of its glow. And Bishop Grange settled down for the night, albeit uneasily. The old clock performed its duty valiantly and conscientiously, ticking sadly as if aware that its demise was drawing near. There was no sound from the library so Harry assumed that the three officers had retired to their rooms.

Harry coughed a little self-consciously, feeling like a tongue-tied schoolboy. He took off his spectacles and polished them, a sure sign that he was playing for time.

"Would you...er...like a drink, Pippa?"

Drawing her knees close up to her chest, she encircled them with her arms and, fingers clasped, rocked backwards and forwards on her slim buttocks. She looked up, her blonde curls tousled and unruly, framing her face, flushed from the last heat of the fire, like a halo. She nodded, her big blue eyes smilingly accepting his offer.

Harry's heart beat wildly. Alone with his love at last. And she, innocent child that she was, would have no notion of the passion that was rising within him. No notion of the desire in his loins, causing the blood to race around his veins. Totally unaware of the frailty of man when faced with such a vision of beauty.

"You want to sleep with me, don't you Harry." It was a statement rather than a question and the boldness of it took him by surprise. He looked around guiltily, half expecting to see Fran leap out of the shadows brandishing a half-eaten sandwich. In spite of his profession having prepared him for all the infidelity, promiscuity and philandering that took place, he was unable to deal with his own unfamiliar yearning for extra marital sex.

But his excitement grew. He had never had sex with anyone except Fran. Trouble was...he didn't know how to start an affair.

"I can't, Harry. I don't cheat you see."

To his surprise, Harry was relieved and there followed a long silence. A companionable silence while they sipped their drinks and watched the logs, spent now and gradually turning to silver grey.

Pippa shivered as she observed the process. Her theatrical mind likened it to Miss Maud's death. Her host had not been kind to her, she thought, but she hadn't deserved to die. What she did deserve was for her killer, should there be one, to be exposed and punished.

"Harry...I read somewhere that for every crime, there must be a matching ...er...ret...ret...ribution."

Harry smiled tenderly, watching her smooth brow wrinkling as she struggled with the word.

"Do you think that's what should happen, Harry?"

"My object all sublime, I shall achieve in time, to let the punishment fit the crime," quoted Harry, softly.

"What do you mean, Harry?"

"I mean...yes Pippa, I do think that's what should happen."

"Harry...I...need to talk to someone. Things have happened. I'm not clever. Not like you. But...I do notice things. And I'm not sure what to do."

"Then leave it until the morning, my dear. We're all tired. Perhaps you'll see things more clearly after a good night's sleep."

"Yes, perhaps you're right. And Leo will be fast asleep now, so there'll be no sex." Her tone was matter of fact, unembarrassed.

"You don't...do you love him?" Harry spoke the word with difficulty. It was a long time since he'd used it.

Pippa stood up, collected her shoes and kissed him gently and briefly on his pale thin lips.

"Of *course* I don't."

....

Harry had been mistaken. Two of the officers were still in the library, DC Brocklebank having excused himself from his superiors, first ascertaining

94

they didn't need his presence any more that night. Inspector Locky had assured him gravely that if, during his discussions with Sergeant McTavish, he felt in need of advice, he would call him. The young detective had looked uncertainly from one to the other, not quite sure if his boss was being sarcastic or not. But no...both men's faces had remained impassive and Brockers finished his beer with a flourish worthy of his idol, Hercule Poirot.

"Right." He'd adopted the word from Locky, using it with the same degree of firmness as his boss, whom he now considered to be his mentor. "If you're sure, then I'll go."

He'd pivoted sharply on one heel as he opened the door, intending to say goodnight, but the two men had already turned their attention back to their beers. Sighing, he left the room, crossed the hall and climbed the stairs, unaware of the unblinking eyes of Hepplewhite ancestors following him. Unaware too, of a pair of tiny black eyes peering from the dining room door. Aggie's eyes. Coal black eyes. Ever watchful. Ever alert. DC Brocklebank's only thought was that if he'd known he was staying overnight, he'd have brought his Agatha Christie book with him. He'd read it once and of course he'd known immediately who the killer was, but he felt it was helping to develop his investigative skills.

....

"Are you really going to take Hepplewhite in, Thomas?" asked Jock, curiously. "You don't think we should wait until we have something from forensic?"

Thomas shook his head. "To tell you the truth, Jock, I don't think there'll be anything from forensic. So many people will have handled that cushion it will be nigh on impossible to pick up anything of any use to us. But...no-one else knows that. So yes, we'll make our move. We can't keep them here much longer, any of them. According to the weather forecast there's going to be a thaw during the night. They'll all start to make their way home."

"What about Tom McCriel? Had the opportunity. And a motive."

Locky shook his head. "Don't think so, Jock. Now the girl, Maggie. Well, she's a different kettle of fish. Protective towards her brother. And a much stronger character of course. In the meantime, I feel we've sufficient grounds to take Leo in for questioning. We'll wait for the medical report though. Make sure she *did* die of suffocation. Hopefully, we'll have that first thing in the morning before anyone stirs. We'd better go to bed. Make an early start tomorrow. What is it, Jock?"

The sergeant placed a finger on his lips, motioning Locky to be quiet. He tiptoed across the room and flung the door open. Stepping quickly outside, he scanned the dimly lit hall. But it was deserted.

He shivered as he re-joined the inspector. Rubbing his hands, he walked over to the fireplace. The fire was almost out although the charcoaled logs were still sending out a little welcome heat.

"I...thought I heard something...er...someone out there."

He turned and stood with his back to the fire and lifted his jacket.

"Tell you the truth sir, I'll be glad to be out of here."

"Oh. Why?"

"Don't know really. It's this house, I suppose. Makes me feel, I don't know...apprehensive. And it smells stale. Old. A bit creepy."

"Well...you don't need to worry Jock. We're sharing a room tonight. I promise I won't let the bogey man get you."

The two men laughed, Locky adjusted the fireguard and they made their way to bed.

....

James was awakened by the sound of dripping water. Sleepily he raised himself on one elbow and turned to look at Alicia. She was still sleeping. Her dark hair fell softly onto her cream-white shoulders, contrasting dramatically with the snow-white fine linen pillowcase as did her thick dark lashes sweeping down on to her pale complexion. He still considered her the most beautiful woman he had ever seen and he was still madly in love with her. She hadn't mentioned having dreamt while she'd been here and James was hoping that, in spite of all the trauma of the weekend, perhaps the break had been good for her. Perhaps he should talk to her again about starting a family. She would be forty-one in a couple of days. Time was moving on. His father would be over the moon if it happened. He quickly dismissed a thought that it also might hasten on his father's decision to make him a partner.

He pulled the old-fashioned counterpane gently over her shoulders and began to ease himself out of bed, stopping and holding his breath as she stirred slightly. It would do her good to sleep. Slipping into a warm woollen dressing gown he silently thanked his father for having suggested they take some warm clothing.

"When them winds blow in from the Penines lad, they'll whip into that old house and round yer arses with the force of an elephant's fart."

James smiled as he recalled his mother's pained expression. She'd never quite come to terms with her husband's occasional lapses back into his native idiom.

"Don't say that in front of Alicia," she'd said.

But for Alicia, his father could do no wrong and James often wondered if he filled a need in her for a father figure. She never spoke of her own father and on one occasion had screamed at him uncontrollably to let the past be when he'd asked about him. James had never mentioned him again.

He moved the curtains to one side, breathing a sigh of relief as he peered out and saw a trickle of melting snow running drunkenly down the window-pane. It would soon be spring. It had been a long, harsh winter and although James knew that more inclement weather was forecast, this morning the snow had almost disappeared, revealing fully now the defiant yellow, white and purple crocus. They held their heads up proudly while the more timid snow-drops bowed theirs, as if giving grateful thanks that their winter duvet had been removed. A cheeky robin cocked his head at James, winking an eye as he hopped around, searching hopefully for a scrap to eat and fighting off any other bird who dared to invade his territory. A bird whose appearance belied its nature. A beautiful but brutal killer.

James shuddered as the full horror of the weekend swept over him. A week-end he'd embarked upon with such high hopes. A weekend in which he had hoped he could prove to his father that he was worthy of a partnership. That he was capable of securing the trust of a client, even one as demanding as Miss Maud. A weekend that had ended in a defenceless woman having the life squeezed out of her by…who? Was it Leo? Or…James could not forget the look on Tom's face as he'd left Maud's bedroom. And he hadn't heard Maud reply. Perhaps she hadn't replied because she was already dead. The threat of being struck off the medical register would be a devastating blow to a doctor after all the years of study. Was this something Tom had been unable to face?

He stepped back from the window, allowing the curtains to fall back into place and the room darkened as the pale early morning light was excluded. Alicia was right. They should leave as soon as possible and never return. He too had seen as much as he wanted of his father's Yorkshire.

Lucy sat on the kitchen table swinging her skinny legs. "What's goin' to 'appen to us Mam?"

"Never mind that now lass. Just you get them fires goin' afore them lot come down."

"They'll not be up for ages yet. That Leo told me not ter ding t'gong."

"Never mind what 'ee sez. You'll ding as usual. We allus ding t'gong when we 'ave guests, yer know that."

"I know. But Mam…'ees boss now. An' he telled me not to."

Her mother sat down wearily, her heavy frame filling the old rocking chair by the side of the Aga, one of the few concessions that Maud had made, albeit reluctantly, to modern living. The old, black kitchen range that it had replaced had been, over the years, the bane of many a cook's life. It now lay discarded in one of the barns, presumably awaiting discovery one day by some enthusiastic collector of kitchenalia.

"Yer right, Lucy. Ah dun't know, bairn. Ah dun't know what's going to 'appen."

Her eyes shone bright with unshed tears. Lucy stared at her mother with dismay as the tears spilled over and ran unchecked down Cook's big apple-red cheeks. She'd never seen her cry before. Unused to any show of affection, Lucy put an arm around her and awkwardly wiped the tears away with the corner of her harsh hessian apron.

"Eee, please Mam. Don't roar. Yer'll start me off."

Clumsily, Cook took the girl in her arms and their tears mingled in joint and noisy despair.

………………………

In a still dark bedroom, other tears were mingling. A brother and sister, tormented by memories of parental abuse, clung together in a desperate attempt to comfort one another.

"I can't bear it Tom, if you have to leave me." Maggie held him tightly. "What will I do? Where will I go? I don't have anyone else."

Tom kissed her cheeks, her salty tears hot on his lips. "I have to speak to the inspector Maggie. We can't live like this any longer. What we're doing is wrong. You know that. And I have to do something about it. I'm the one to blame. I should never have let things go so far. You'd better go back to your room, darling."

After his sister had left, Tom McCriel buried his head deep into the pillow to stifle his sobs, bitterly regretting having acceded to Maud's demands that he go and see her.

Chapter Sixteen

James and Alicia stood in the hallway, packed suitcases by their side, waiting for Inspector Locky.

"Are you sure you don't want anything to eat, Alicia?" asked James anxiously. "We've a long journey ahead of us."

"Stop fussing James." Alicia, dressed in the green tweed suit she had arrived in, draped a matching cape over her shoulders. "Let's get the hell out of here. I think I can honestly say this has been the most disastrous weekend I have ever spent in my whole life. We can stop on the road for something to eat."

James glanced at his watch. "It's only seven. I don't know what time he'll be coming down."

"James, for God's sake. Can't we just go? We don't need permission, do we?"

"No Mrs Brent. You don't."

The pair turned around, startled. Standing with their backs to the staircase, they hadn't heard the inspector coming down the stairs.

"I am, however, requesting that you *do* stay. Our inquiries aren't yet complete. And they would be made much simpler if the whole party remained in one place. In Bishop Grange. Of course, I can't *compel* anyone to stay, but…"

"How long?" demanded Alicia, impatiently.

"As long as it takes," replied Inspector Locky, mildly.

"I'd better ring my father to let him know what's happened. Of course we'll stay, Inspector. Alicia, we may as well have breakfast. I'll take the cases back upstairs."

"Those cases have been up and down like yo-yos, James. And…I don't want anything to eat. I don't suppose, Inspector, you'll object if I go outside for a while?" She began pulling on a pair of leather gloves, indicating that she didn't much care whether he objected or not.

The inspector smiled and shook his head. "Certainly not, madam." His eyes had been drawn to her long slender fingers. That's a beautiful ring you have, Mrs Brent. The solitaire I mean. One to be looked after, I'll be bound. Hope you have it well insured."

"Yes, it is," said James. "Although she….." he stopped quickly. He'd been going to say that she was a bit careless with it and had very nearly lost it this weekend. He could see the inspector was not over impressed with her, but James was proud of her and didn't want her to be thought of as a stupid woman who couldn't look after her belongings.

"Hang about darling. I'll come with you."

"Please, James. Can't I be on my own for five minutes? Stop mollycoddling me. You go and have breakfast." She turned sharply on her heel and flounced majestically out of the front door.

James laughed self-consciously. "She's an independent lady, I'm afraid, Inspector."

The inspector smiled at him sympathetically. "Don't apologise Mr Brent. Nothing wrong in being independent and I suppose this has been a pretty traumatic experience for all of you. Not…quite what you expected it to be, eh?"

"Oh *there* you are, Inspector." Fran approached him with a worried look on her face. "Do you think we shall be able to go home today? If not, I shall have to make some arrangements about laundry. Harry has run out of clean shirts and I've run out of…well…all sorts of things."

"I think we can expect to draw events to a satisfactory conclusion today, Mrs Gough."

"That's good," said Fran, with a relieved sigh. "I *knew* it must have all been a dreadful mistake. I suppose poor Maud had a heart attack. I'm so glad it's all turned out alright. And it's my bridge night at the golf club tonight. *What* a story I shall have to tell them."

"In that case, Mrs Gough," smiled the inspector, "It would be very cruel of me to keep you. I wouldn't want to deprive you of that pleasure."

Fran beamed. "I'll go and see if there's a bit of breakfast. Not that I can eat much first thing in the morning. Is anyone else coming in?"

"Morning all."

"Ah, Brocklebank. Go wait in the library. I'm expecting a 'phone call."

Fran re-appeared from the dining room. "There's no breakfast. And the table's not been laid. I wonder if Cook's ill? Ah, here's Leo. Leo…there's no breakfast."

"What do you mean, no breakfast?" Leo, warmly dressed in a bright red polo-necked sweater which emphasised his bull neck, joined the group in the hall. "Why is everyone standing in here?" He flung open the sitting-room door. "And there's no bloody fire either. Where the hell's all the staff?"

Fran patted his arm soothingly. "Don't get in a state, Leo. I'll go and see what's wrong"

"Inspector, can I have a word, please?" Tom McCriel touched the inspector's arm.

"Jesus," scowled Leo, causing his walrus moustache to droop even further. "It's like Piccadilly bloody Circus here. Shall I be glad to get back to London to some sanity. Where's Aggie? She'll get me something to eat."

"Come into the library Mr McCriel," said the inspector softly, opening the library door. "Out, Brockers."

"But sir, what about the telephone call?"

"I said *out,* Brocklebank."

Fran poked her head round the kitchen door. Lucy was standing helplessly by the Aga with a rasher of bacon dangling from her fingers.

"Where's Cook this morning Lucy?"

"She's gone back ter bed. I dun't know where ter start. I've niver cooked on mi own before. Me Mam's always dun it."

"What's wrong with your Mam, Lucy? Is she ill?"

"No. Me Mam's never badly. She's just mithering about what's going to 'appen to us." Her thin shoulders shook with desperate sobs. "So am I. We've got nowhere ter go if that Mr Leo chucks us out."

"Where's Aggie?"

Lucy shook her head. "Not seen 'er this mornin' yet."

"Move over. And stop sniffling. Pass your Mam's apron over."

Lucy stopped crying and watched with interest as Fran discarded the blue cardigan, so artlessly admired by Pippa, and covered her ill-fitting skirt with Cook's voluminous apron. Fran had long since ceased trying to buy skirts that actually fitted. To her, they were now merely covering agents, but she did take pride in her twin-sets which she knitted incessantly, an activity which drove Harry to despair.

"Can yer cook then?" asked a surprised Lucy.

"Of course I can cook," laughed Fran. "I don't have servants at home, Lucy. Harry…Mr Gough, is a solicitor, not a wealthy land owner. Come on Lucy. Move yourself. We'll just have bacon and eggs this morning."

Her tears forgotten, Lucy chatted animatedly, unaccustomed to the novelty of a guest cooking breakfast.

"You'll be well off though, won't yer? So…'ow do yer get to be a solicitor then?"

"Pass me some more bacon. You'd better go and set the table."

Lucy repeated her question. "*How* though?"

Fran stopped cooking, holding the spatula high in the air and looked at the girl speculatively. "How did you do at school, Lucy?"

Lucy shrugged her shoulders. "Alright. I wanted to stay on for a bit but me Mam said it war a waste o' time. I liked English. And 'istory. Me teacher were right mad when I left."

Fran looked at her with some sadness. Same old story, she thought. Although she had never pursued a career, she'd had the choice. And she had chosen to marry early. Be a home-maker. She doubted that this little girl would ever have that choice.

"Best go an'do t'table, lass."

"Eee, yer sound just like me Mam. Mind you, she'd 'ave clipped me round t'lug-ole by now."

Fran dipped a slice of bread into the sizzling bacon fat and handed it to her, laughing at the girl's doleful expression. "So will I Lucy, if yer dun't gerra move on. Lucy..."

Fran hesitated, unable to decide if she should speak to the girl about her education. Best not. She might only unsettle her and incur her mother's wrath for interfering.

Lucy, sensing a sympathetic spirit, smiled at her as she stuffed the succulent morsel of bread and hot dripping into her mouth. Fran felt her heart lurch. Why...she was a beautiful girl. How she would have loved a child like this. Her mind made up, she patted Lucy's arm.

"You and I will have a little chat, dear. Now, wipe your hands and face and get on with that table."

....

Inspector Locky and Tom McCriel came out of the library, both looking grim. As they did the telephone rang.

"I'll speak to you later Mr McCriel. Brocklebank, find Sergeant McTavish. Tell him to get his arse in here. Sharp, lad."

The inspector closed the door carefully behind him and strode purposefully to the telephone. The library door opened and his sergeant entered. Locky waved at him impatiently to close the door as he listened intently to the voice at the other end of the telephone.

"Right. Yes. Is the Chief in yet? No, it doesn't matter. I'll do the necessary at this end."

Sergeant McTavish watched with interest, trying to glean some information from his boss's expression, but it remained inscrutable.

Placing the telephone back on its cradle, Inspector Locky spoke. "That was the doc. Maud was murdered all right. Found traces of velvet on her face and pressure had been applied. She was suffocated. Didn't even struggle."

"Did you speak to McCriel, Thomas?" asked the Sergeant.

"Yes."

The sergeant waited. He knew better than to make any comment at this stage. He tried to guess at the conversation between his boss and the young doctor. Had it changed his decision to take in Leo? Tom McCriel had had the opportunity and certainly a motive.

The inspector walked across the room to the window and stood, his back tense as he gazed with unseeing eyes at the rustic scene outside. A couple of pheasants stepped daintily across the last diminishing patches of snow on the lawn in front of the house, looking like two decorous young ladies out for a morning stroll and a gaggle of geese strutted contentedly behind them. One of the ginger farm cats studiously ignored the deceptively docile geese, judiciously giving them a wide berth. It chased away a solitary deer which had been looking nervously over its shoulder as it walked almost to the front door, then pounced on a mouse which had mistakenly thought the cat was otherwise engaged. It lay on its back, tail swaying from side to side in sheer ecstasy as it allowed the terrified mouse to escape so far and no further, before pawing it back with feline indolence. A nest of rabbits raced around in seemingly aimless changes of direction until one raised its tail, showing the warning white fur and then all disappeared to the safety of their burrow.

But Inspector Locky saw none of this country activity. His agile investigative mind was rapidly turning over the events that had been relayed to him. As his shoulders remained hunched, his sergeant watched in sympathetic silence. The waiting continued for several more minutes. Then the inspector straightened up, drawing back his shoulders as if a heavy burden had been lifted from them.

"Right."

And Sergeant McTavish stood mentally to attention. He knew a decision had been made.

Chapter Seventeen

DC Brocklebank stood to attention outside the dining room door, aware that important decisions were being made by his superiors. The young detective had an exaggerated sense of drama when an arrest was imminent. He was determined to make a name for himself on the back of this case. He still had to live down the night when, as a uniformed constable, he'd allowed a burglar to relieve him of his handcuffs and truncheon. The burglar had then hit him over the head with it and fastened him to the door handle with the handcuffs. To add insult to injury, the burglar had rung the police station to tell them where to find their beat bobby. It was shortly after this he'd been promoted to CID and there were still whispered suggestions of nepotism floating around the station. There were recollections amongst the older members of the force of a young civilian typist leaving shortly after a Christmas party and DC Brocklebank did strongly resemble one of the hierarchy in the force.

But young Brocklebank was blissfully unaware of the gossip that surrounded him and was convinced that, if he kept his nose clean, he would rise to at least Chief Inspector.

"Stay at that door," the inspector had said. "Our suspect might make a dash for it. And if you cock it up, you'll be back on the beat before you can say 'Hercule Poirot'."

"Who is it sir?" he asked eagerly.

But the inspector and sergeant had already gone in to the dining room.

"Stand by the door, Jock," whispered the inspector quietly.

Maggie and Tom were sitting, not together as usual, but facing one another at the table, as were Pippa and Harry. Leo had taken his place at the head of the table, making his position in the household clear to everyone. James was holding the door open for Fran as she bustled in and out with bacon and eggs, followed by Lucy bearing racks of toast.

"Are you ready for yours Inspector? I'll go and put more bacon on. My goodness, I'm glad I don't have to do this every day. Well, not for this many people."

"Never mind that now Mrs Gough. Come and sit down please. You too Lucy."

Fran stopped in her tracks suddenly as she recognized the gravity in Inspector Locky's voice.

"I have just had a call from the police surgeon supporting Lucy's statement that she found Miss Maud with the cushion over her face. They found particles of the cushion around Maud's lips and inside her nose. I have to tell you that this appears to confirm that someone held the cushion over her face until she stopped breathing. I have to tell you that Miss Maud was murdered."

"Oh, my God." There was a clatter as Fran dropped the plate of bacon. Maggie reached across the table and took hold of Tom's hand.

"See. I telt yer." Lucy's voice was triumphant. "I weren't tellin' lies."

James strode across the dining room towards the door, only to be confronted by Sergeant McTavish.

"Sorry sir. I can't let you leave I'm afraid."

"Where do you think you're going Mr Brent?" asked the inspector. The roughness in his voice caused James to turn back in surprise.

"I must go and find my wife. If there's a killer on the loose...well...she's out there alone."

"Stay where you are sir, if you don't mind."

It was clear from Inspector Locky's authoritative tones that he wasn't asking him. He was telling him. James sat down meekly.

"I don't think we need worry about a killer being outside Mr Brent."

The significance of his remark and his steely gaze travelling around the table, pausing for a second on each person, sent a shiver up the spine of each and every one of them.

DC Brocklebank strained his ears at the door, vainly trying to hear the name of the suspect and Sergeant McTavish issued a silent prayer to his Maker, fervently requesting that Thomas' instincts wouldn't let him down.

A breathless hush descended in the room. The steady, tick-tock of the old long-case clock sent its inexorable message of passing time. A steady plop of water fell on to the windowsill with irritating regularity whilst a rush of melting snow slithered like a loud whisper down the roof. A faint but frantic scratching in the wainscot suggested that a mouse had assumed that the silence meant solitude.

"Mr Hepplewhite...Leo Hepplewhite, I must ask you to accompany me to the station for further questioning in connection with the death of your cousin, Miss Maud Hepplewhite."

For a few seconds there was a shocked silence. Even though everyone, except Pippa, had had their suspicions, having them confirmed filled them with a sense of unreality, as if someone was going to burst into the room and shout 'April Fool'.

There was a shout. A crazed prolonged shout, akin to the bellowing of a wounded elephant. And Leo took hold of the end of the table, thrusting it away from him with such force it toppled over, emptying its load of half eaten bacon and eggs and scalding hot tea into the laps of the alarmed company.

"Let me get at her. I'll kill her."

Harry instinctively held out a protective hand towards Pippa, but Leo's outburst was not directed at his lover. He headed with astonishing speed and agility for a man with his bulk, towards a surprised Lucy.

"She killed her. *She* put the bleeding cushion over her."

Two racks of toast flew into the air as Lucy squealed and ran to the door where Sergeant McTavish, stunned by the unexpected turn of events, stood rooted to the floor.

"Mam. Mam," she wailed, as she struggled with the door-handle.

DC Brocklebank, waiting patiently outside, obligingly turned it.

"Stop her," roared Leo.

With a rugby tackle that would have delighted a Twickenham crowd, DC Brocklebank brought Lucy to the ground, her thin arms and legs flailing ineffectively beneath the weight of the young detective.

Sergeant McTavish, his composure restored, grasped Leo and, with the help of his boss, manacled his wrists behind his back.

"Just for questioning sir," murmured the inspector soothingly.

"And Brockers," he said in a deceptively mild and controlled voice, "piss off back to the station and take a fortnight's leave." He bared his teeth in an ominous smile. "For so help me, if I have to see your face in the next few days, I'll kick your arse so hard your balls will hit the ceiling."

Lucy, unexpectedly released from the weight of a bemused young detective, ran up the stairs with the speed of a frightened gazelle.

Back in the dining room, Maggie and Tom McCriel leaned back in their chairs, breathing tremulous sighs of relief. Fran fussed over Pippa who was sobbing uncontrollably whilst Harry looked on, his eyes watering as he listened to the girl's distraught cries. James, concerned about Alicia, shuffled uncomfortably in his chair.

"Harry."

Harry reluctantly switched his eyes from Pippa to James.

"Hmm. Yes James?"

"Do you think I could go out now and find my wife?"

"I don't see why not." He removed his spectacles and began to slowly polish them. "I expect we shall all be going home shortly. The inspector has our addresses for when we are needed."

Pippa sobbed even more copiously at the mention of home.

"I haven't got a home now, Harry. I've nowhere to go. I don't know what to do."

Harry stared at her with an anguished expression on his face.

"You shall stay with us for the time being," said Fran firmly. "That's all right Harry, isn't it?"

"Whatever you say my dear, " replied Harry mildly, his heart thumping wildly as he replaced his spectacles. "Whatever you say."

Lucy burst into her mother's room with the speed of a tornado. "They've taken that Leo away Mam."

Cook was lying on her bed, her starched white apron over her face. "*Mr* Leo, Lucy. Watch yer tongue girl," she said, struggling to sit upright. "What yer mean Lucy? Taken 'im where?"

"To t'bobbyole," said Lucy excitedly, her fear now abated. "It were 'im. 'Ee dun 'er in. Cum on Mam, gerrup. I want ter see what 'appens next. An' Mam, 'ee tried to say it were me that dun it."

Cook shot up like a piston, her fear of what the future held for them completely superseded by the suggestion that her girl was guilty of murder.

"Did 'ee now? 'Ow dare 'ee?" she exploded indignantly. "'Ere…" she lowered her voice, "yer didn't did yer?"

Lucy ignored the remark and turned to leave the room. "I'll go an' tell Aggie."

But Lucy did not have to tell Aggie. Aggie had seen Leo being taken away. And she'd moaned softly, her tired and wrinkled old face crumbling as she'd heard the news. She'd moved swiftly back to her room and, opening the closet door, selected a severe black coat and bonnet from her meagre wardrobe. She put them on quickly, opened the top drawer in the pine dressing table and lifted the lid of a black velvet-covered box. She stared at the scant contents with tiny, black, expressionless eyes.

A yellowing, much handled letter from her mother informing her of her father's death in an accident, the only letter her mother had ever written to her. A few pieces of cheap costume jewellery, a faded photograph of Miss Maud's mother, Sarah, a lock of dark hair, a photograph of a baby lying naked on its belly, a tiny milk tooth and a long silver hat pin with a mother-of-pearl knob.

Aggie picked up the latter, her gnarled fingers handling the object with some difficulty. A slight flicker of her eyes betrayed some sign of poignant recollection. It had been a present from Sarah Hepplewhite when...Aggie's eyes quickly reverted back to the apparently unseeing gaze of a servant, as she regained control of deeply buried and long forgotten emotions. Without looking in the mirror she stuck the pin into the back of her bonnet and scooped up a large handbag and an old fashioned brolly with a tortoise shell handle, one of Miss Maud's cast-offs. Without a backward glance at the tiny room that had been her secure and insular space for the past fifty-seven years, she walked resolutely into the passage and down the stairs.

Chapter Eighteen

"So, Thomas, are you doing anything about the brother and sister?" Sergeant McTavish, relaxing back at the station with a cup of canteen coffee grimaced as the bitterness permeated his taste buds. "Christ. We could do worse than offer a job here to the Hepplewhite Cook. She makes a good cuppa. Wonder what will happen to her."

"Poor Lily," mused Inspector Locky sadly. "Not much job security there, is there? And Aggie. Who will want her now? Hopefully, Maud will have made some provision for the poor sods."

"So," persisted his sergeant. "What about the McCriels? Are you going to tell me what Tom McCriel wanted to see you about? I wondered if he was about to confess to the killing."

The inspector laughed. "Come on Jock. You've been in the force long enough to know we don't get things handed to us on a plate as easily as that. Although, I must admit I did wonder. No, he came to ask me the same as you. What was I going to do about it? Are they going to be facing incest charges? They're worried sick about losing their jobs, obviously. I told him...I'm doing nothing. It's the father I'd like to do something about, but neither of them want any action taking. And they could of course, as you know, even after all this time. He's promised it will end. And I believe him. His sister doesn't know yet but he's decided to go to Australia. Had it in mind for a while. The girl will be devastated. And she's the strong one. He's a weak character yet he's the one that's prepared to do something about it. Terrible thing this child abuse, isn't it? Those two are perfect examples of the damage it does. In the meantime, let's see if we can break our Mr Leo, shall we? And...it's my turn to be Mr Nice Guy."

"He'll take some convincing of that, Thomas," laughed Jock.

The canteen door opened and the two men groaned.

"Thought I told you to bugger off, Brockers," said the inspector quietly, somewhat mollified by having pulled someone in for the job.

Unperturbed, DC Brocklebank smirked triumphantly. "Couldn't be spared this week. Message for you sir. It seems Aggie is wanting to speak to you. She's sitting on the doorstep at Bishop Grange. Won't move till she's seen you. Wants you back there. And sir...she says you're to bring back Leo." Lulled into a false sense of security by his boss's mild tone, he added. "At once."

The young constable shut the door hastily as two cups of putrid coffee were hurled at it.

....

"I can't do anything with her." Fran shook her head and looked around the sitting room helplessly. "Says she won't come in until she's seen Inspector Locky. It's *freezing* out there. Harry, see if she'll listen to you."

Pippa, who had lit a fire earlier rose from her knees and wiped her hands down the side of trim fitting trousers. "I think the logs are a bit damp but it should burn all right now. Shall I come out with you Harry? We can't leave her out there. It's starting to snow very heavily again."

"Oh no," groaned Alicia. "James, are we *never* going to get home?"

"Shall I make some coffee?" Maggie took hold of her brother's hands and attempted to pull him out of the chair. "Come on Tom, you can help." Tom shook his hands free. "No Maggie. No."

He spoke sharply and Maggie stared at him, hurt by the unaccustomed tone of his voice.

"No Maggie," he smiled at her and spoke softly now. "You do it."

"Mi Mam's better. She sez does anybody want a drink?" Lucy's head poked round the door. "An' there's a police car comin' up t'drive."

....

"Jesus," groaned Inspector Locky. "Look at this Jock. Have you ever seen a more pathetic sight?"

As the police car drove slowly towards the house Aggie came into full view. She was sitting on the front doorstep, her lips set tightly in mute stoicism, her wide-brimmed bonnet slightly askew, gripping her brolly and handbag with grim determination and looking for all the world like an aged Mary Poppins.

The car had barely stopped before Locky jumped out and gently lifted her tiny frame from the cold stone step.

"Now then lass," he said gently. "What's all this about? You'll catch your death of cold out here. Let's get you inside shall we?"

Aggie meekly allowed herself to be propelled indoors. Locky, now a compassionate gentle giant, pushed open the sitting room door and almost carried her towards the fire.

"Give her some space," he whispered to the others. "And some time."

"You've brought 'im back, 'ave yer sir?" she asked pitifully.

Locky hesitated. "Can't do that, Aggie. He has to answer some questions first, I'm afraid."

She stared into the fire. "He's got nowt ter tell yer. He'd nowt ter do wi' it."

She turned her head slowly towards him, her tiny black eyes seeking his and she began to speak, her voice firm and strong.

"Mr Leo didn't kill Miss Maud. You must let him go, Inspector."

Pippa was the first to notice. Aggie's strong Yorkshire accent was barely discernable. As if all those years of living with Hepplewhites had suddenly and unexpectedly had its effect. As if for the first time in her life, Aggie had something important to say. And for the first time, she knew that someone was going to listen to her.

"Why do you say that, Aggie?"

"Because, Inspector Locky...I killed her. I killed Miss Maud."

An ominous quiet settled on the stunned party like a cloud of fine dust, so fine it could only be felt, not seen.

They waited for the inspector to dismiss Aggie's statement as the rantings of a disturbed and overwrought old woman. They waited for him to comfort her. Pat her tiny head and send her to bed with a hot drink, telling her she'd feel better in the morning.

"When, Aggie? When did you do it? What time was it? Why Aggie? Why did you kill her?" He fired question after question at her, like shots from a pistol.

"Inspector. *Really*." Fran interrupted his interrogation reprovingly. "I think you're being a bit harsh, aren't you?"

"That'll do, Fran." Harry rebuked her sharply and the inspector nodded his thanks.

"Perhaps Aggie, we'd best ask everyone to leave, shall we?"

"No Inspector."

She spoke with an authority and a clarity that left them all stunned.

"I'll tell all of them. They should know. It's time everyone knew. I *did* kill Miss Maud. Just before Lucy brought her tea. I took the cushion from her wheel chair. It...was very dark. The curtains were still drawn, you see. I walked across to the bed, closed my eyes and pressed the cushion on her face. She never moved. Never moved at all. Poor Miss Maud. Poor lass."

Aggie stopped speaking. Tears began to trickle down her cheeks, following the deep lines in her face. The clock chimed intrusively, as if demanding that she continue with her revelations.

Pippa began to speak. "But..." and was silenced by a frown from Harry. Lucy, who had been listening outside the door ran into the kitchen.

"Mam...Mam. Yer'd better cum in ter t'sitting room. Something 'orrible is 'appening."

"Never mind what's 'appening in there. You just keep yer mind on what's 'appenin' in 'ere. We've gorra job ter look after, me an' you. Now, grab 'old of that coffee."

"Never mind t'coffee." Lucy grabbed hold of her mother's hand impatiently. "It's Aggie. She needs us."

Without further ado, Cook wiped her hands on her apron and marched out of the kitchen, across the hall and into the sitting room.

"Why, Aggie?" asked Sergeant McTavish sadly. "Why did you do it?"

Inspector Locky stayed silent. And waited. Everyone remained quiet, scarcely daring to breathe.

"Had to. I heard Miss Maud that night. Telling Mr Leo that she would change her will. That he wouldn't get Bishop Grange. That weren't right, see. It's his. By right. As much as it were hers. I couldn't let her do that to my Leo. He's mine you see. My babby. I'm his Mam."

And then she cried. Silently at first, then with increasing volume. Her narrow shoulders, racked with harsh sobs shook and her body trembled as years of pent up emotions were released.

Sergeant McTavish turned away. He needed to blow his nose. Must be starting a cold, he told himself.

Cook moved to her side and gently took her by the hand. She allowed herself to be seated in a large leather chair, her tiny body appearing incongruous in its masculine imagery.

"Get 'er a brandy," demanded Cook. "Go on," she shouted, as everyone stared transfixed at Aggie. "Get er a drink."

Harry dutifully moved toward the drinks cabinet. "Yes Cook. Yes, I think, perhaps we could all do with a little something."

"I'll 'ave a port an' lemon." Lucy settled herself down in the corner of a settee in gleeful anticipation.

"You'll gerrin that kitchen an' scrape them spuds. This int fer your ears. Now Aggie luv. You tell Cook all about it."

Lucy, ignoring her mother's command, held her breath and pressed her body deeper into the settee as if she by doing so she would be inconspicuous.

112

Lucy had no intention of being tucked away from all the excitement. Aggie's sobs gradually subsided and she began to speak again.

"I was only fifteen. I'd been here some eighteen months. The Master…Mr George…well, I never saw him much. He was nearly always away. The Missus…she were that good to me. I loved her more than anybody else in the 'ole world. More than my own Mam. She were pregnant with Miss Grace, Miss Maud's little sister that was. One night, the Master got drunk. Well…more than usual. I heard him and the Missus rowing something awful. Then he came to my room. Said I had to be a good girl and be nice to him. I knew what he meant, me being the eldest of six kids. Not much is kept private in a two up an' two down. He said if I didn't…you know…he'd 'ave me sent away. Well, mi Mam couldn't have me back an' she needed the money and I'd no where else to go. An' anyway, Missus needed me here. So I just shut me eyes an' let 'im gerron wi' it." As Aggie's voice became more and more agitated, her native vernacular returned. "He 'urt me somethin' awful. I thought I were gunna split. I niver telt a soul. It were t'Missus that saw I were goin' to 'ave a bairn. So I 'ad to tell 'er."

She began to cry again and Cook held the glass of brandy to her lips. She drank it and shuddered as the strong pungent liquor burned her throat, but the effect of the unaccustomed alcohol quickly helped her recover her composure.

"She sent me away. The Master's brother, Mr Ernest and his wife, they lived in Whitby. She couldn't 'ave any bairns so, when mine came they just…kept him. And I came back to Bishop Grange. I were lucky though really. I saw him a lot when he was little. I loved it when he came to stay. His dad…well, who he thought were his dad, Mr Ernest, he died when Leo…Mr Leo were young. The Master…his real dad, didn't want owt to do with 'im when he came 'ere. Like as if he were ashamed of 'im. That really 'urt me. But the missus treated 'im well. He used to play with Miss Maud and Miss Grace. He never knew they were his half-sisters." She paused, her eyes filling with tears again. "And he niver knew that I were 'is mam. So yer see, I couldn't let him be cheated could I? Not me own bairn. This is his house. My Leo's inheritance."

Chapter Nineteen

"Inspector."

Inspector Locky stopped and turned around, to see Pippa running after him. Her young breasts, their contours hugged by a cornflower blue sweater exactly the same colour as her eyes, jigged up and down as she ran and he quickly averted his eyes from the fascinating motion. Sergeant McTavish had gone on ahead, escorting Aggie to the police car by gently holding her arm, more protective than custodial. His boss had been following, deep in thought, a few yards behind.

"Please Inspector. I *must* speak to you."

"Not now Miss," sighed the inspector. "I really can't discuss Leo Hepplewhite with you at the moment."

"It's not about Leo. Well...not directly. It's about Aggie."

"Look...Miss...this has been a long and tiring day. And it's only one-o-clock. I am cold, weary, hungry," his voice began to rise alarmingly "and I've got to put a seventy year old woman through one hell of a time. So please...don't bother me eh. Just...go away. I'm sure you'll see your boyfriend again before very long."

His tone became sarcastic and Pippa, her hackles rising, screamed at him.

"You must listen Inspector. There's something I can do. And there's only me can do it. If I don't, I'll never forgive myself. Please...just let me talk, will you?"

Inspector Locky stared at her intently. There was an urgency, a sincerity in her voice that stirred something inside him. That something that singled out the wheat from the chaff. Singled out a good detective from a run-of the mill copper. Something called gut feeling. A tingling in the veins that told him this could be important.

Grabbing her arm firmly, he marched her back to the house.

"This'd better be good," he said firmly. "Lily," he snapped at a startled Cook. "Coffee. Pronto. In the library."

....

"No James. I'm sorry. If you won't leave now, I shall take the car and go home by myself. I am determined not to spend one more night in this house."

"Alicia, be reasonable. You're placing me in a very difficult position. We can't go yet. Aggie's confession has changed everything. We're not going until Inspector Locky says we can."

"And I'm afraid I'm going to have to ask you all to be patient. Just a little while longer, Mrs Brent." Inspector Locky smiled pleasantly as he entered the sitting room. "Mrs Gough, I wonder if I could have a word. In the library, if you please."

Fran looked up, startled. "A word, Inspector. With me? I'm…sure I've told you all I know."

She looked flustered and James watched the inspector with interest. What was the old dog up to, he wondered? He surely didn't think Fran had anything to do with the murder. Surely Aggie's confession was the end of it. He began to ponder. What if Harry was a beneficiary in Miss Maud's will. Fran would know. Perhaps they were short of cash. And Miss Maud had threatened to change her will. What if she'd intended not only to cut out Leo, but everyone else as well? What if Aggie was lying about having killed Miss Maud merely to protect Leo? What if…he gave himself a shake. This place was beginning to get to him. He was beginning to suspect everyone.

"Only to clear up one or two points, Mrs Gough. Nothing to worry about, I assure you."

The inspector smiled at her benignly. But James noted that the smile did not reach his eyes. They remained as cold as flint. Sharp and searching. And James suddenly recognized the nature of the man. Inspector Locky would search relentlessly until he found what he was looking for.

…………………..

"I suppose we'll 'ave to cook for 'em all again tonight Mam."

"Ee Lucy luv. I cud really do wi'out all o' them. I'm that upset about Aggie."

"Do yer think she *really* did it Mam?" Lucy sat on the kitchen table swinging her skinny legs.

Her mother eyed her critically. "You mi girl, could do wi' a bit o' meat on yer. I dun't know lass. She sez she did. Mebbee she did an' mebbee she didn't."

"Mebbee I tek after mi Dad." Lucy squinted slyly at her mother. "Were 'e skinny?"

"Nowt to do wi' you."

"Course it's summat ter do wi'me." Lucy jumped down from the table indignantly. "I might be a lady. I could be royalty from what yer've telt me about that place yer worked. Cum on, Mam. Tell us. Were it the Maister?"

Lucy bobbed and curtsied sarcastically. "Did his Lordship 'av 'is wicked way wi' yer? Like dirty old 'Epplewhite did wi' Aggie? Aahh, that 'urt."

Lucy ducked out of reach as her mother raised her hand to deliver a second blow.

"I will tell you this, *mother* dear." Lucy spoke slowly and deliberately. "I will not spend mi life doin' for other folk. I've seen the other side. I've seen another life style. I'll be somebody I will. Just you wait and see."

"Aye… I'll wait an' see. An' if yer must know, Miss 'igh an' mighty, yer dad were an 'igh class purveyor of animals."

"The game-keeper?" asked Lucy eagerly.

"No," replied her mother. "The butcher."

....

"Well, that's alright then." Fran beamed as she re-joined her companions. "All cleared up."

"Has anyone seen Pippa?"

"What do you want her for Harry?"

"Nothing dear." Harry shrugged his shoulders nonchalantly. "Just wondered where she was."

"Do you want to go for a walk, Tom?" Maggie looked at her brother pleadingly. "I feel as if I've been cooped up here for years. I really could do with a breather."

Tom raised his eyes from the magazine. "I don't think so, Maggie. I…want to finish this article in here, if you don't mind. Perhaps Alicia will go with you."

"No thank you, Tom." Alicia leaned towards him languidly and slowly turned his magazine the right way up. Tom flushed and placed it back in the rack.

"Ah, here she is." Harry smiled as Pippa entered the room. "We were concerned about you, my dear."

"Tom, you will remember to let me have the name of that…what was it again?"

"Chiropractor, Mrs Gough," sighed Tom.

"Oh do call me Fran. I feel we all know one another so well. Yes, that's it. Chiropractor. Harry, you'll remember that for me won't you?"

"Yes dear," sighed Harry.

"Is your back still bothering you, Fran?" inquired Pippa, looking concerned.

"Oh my dear. I'm a *martyr* to my back, am I not, Harry?"

"Yes dear," agreed Harry fervently. "A martyr indeed."

"Fran…" began Pippa slowly. "No…no, you'd never let me."

"Let you what, dear?"

"Hypnotise you."

There followed an incredulous silence.

"Hypnotise. *You.*" Alicia began to laugh. " You're a bird-brain. What do you know about hypnosis?"

"That's a rather pernicious remark, Mrs Brent," said Harry, his pale thin lips drawn tightly over his teeth. "Quite uncalled for."

"That's alright, Harry," said Pippa seriously. "I know it must seem rather odd but I do actually know what I'm doing."

"Well, if you're sure." Fran looked around the room apprehensively.

"Positive," replied Pippa confidently. "I may be a bird-brain in some respects but I wouldn't mess about with hypnosis if I wasn't competent. I had a good teacher. Best in the business, as it happens. He was a doctor. Well, had been. Well, still is really, I suppose. I can help you relax you see. And that very often helps. In fact Fran, I could teach you self hypnosis for when the pain starts again."

"Take care, Pippa," warned Tom.

She flashed him a reassuring smile. "Don't worry."

"Come and sit on the settee Fran. Alicia, would you mind sitting with her, just for a bit of moral support?"

Alicia hesitated for a couple of seconds then moved to the settee, shrugging her shoulders. "OK. Anything to relieve the boredom."

"Alicia, no. Look I really don't like this." James shook his head. "I won't let you. It could do you some damage."

"James, please. Don't tell me what I can or can't do. Anyway, it's Fran that should be worried."

Pippa looked around her, very much in charge now. "Will you all remain seated please. And can I ask that no one speaks. No matter what happens." She knelt in front of the women and smiled at them. "Don't be afraid, Fran. Just relax. You're only going to sleep. A deep, a *very* deep sleep. You will remain aware of everything that's happening but you will hear only *my* voice. Nothing else but my voice. Close your eyes if you want. It's so quiet. And peaceful. Relax your toes. That's good."

Pippa's voice was soft yet persuasive. Gentle yet authoritative, developing a crooning quality. And everyone recognized that the girl had not made any false claims. She was indeed a competent operator.

"And now your fingers. Your legs are heavy. They're getting heavier. Now they're relaxing. Now they're light. You can float if you want to. Your body's tingling and it's pleasant. I'm going to count. I'm going to count to ten. By then you'll be fast asleep but you'll still hear me. Only me." Pippa began to count slowly. The only other sound in the room came from the old clock whose pendulum took up the challenge, assisting Pippa by swinging alternatively with Pippa's steady count, providing an additional hypnotic atmosphere.

By the count of eight, the rhythm of both Fran *and* Alicia's breathing had changed. It had slowed down discernibly. It was steady and even. The muscles in their faces relaxed. Fran's cheeks were flushed in contrast to Alicia's. Hers were deathly pale. Their eyelids began to flutter rapidly. Pippa watched them intently for a couple of minutes and then she rose, turning to James, shrugging her shoulders apologetically.

He stared at her wild-eyed. "What have you done?" he asked in a strangled voice.

She placed a finger on her lips and turned back to Alicia. "You can hear me, Alicia?"

Alicia nodded.

"Are you comfortable? Speak Alicia."

"Alicia, you don't have to tell me anything you don't want to tell me. Do you understand that?"

"Yes."

"You have a dream, Alicia. A dream that keeps coming back. Do you know why?"

"I don't know why?"

"Do you want to know?"

"Yes."

"Why do you want to know?"

"Because it frightens me."

Pippa knelt in front of her again and took hold of her hand. "Alicia, I want

118

you to think back to when you were a little girl. When you lived with your Mum and Dad. In Yorkshire."

There was a sharp intake of breath from behind Pippa, but she continued undeterred.

"You were born in Yorkshire weren't you, Alicia?"

Alicia's eyelids fluttered frantically and she hesitated slightly before replying. "Yes."

"You know this house don't you, Alicia?"

Again, an almost imperceptible pause. "Yes."

"Tell me," urged Pippa.

A long silence followed and then Alicia began to speak, faltering at first, and then with increasing confidence.

"We lived in a tiny cottage, one in a row of ten. My dad worked in the pit, but we never had any money. I think he put it on the horses. And he played cards a lot. We had a back yard with a lavvy. I hated that. There were mice and things."

Alicia shuddered and James rose from the chair towards her.

"Stop this, Pippa."

Harry stepped forward and gently took hold of his arm.

"Leave her, James. I'm sure Pippa knows what she's doing."

Pippa, ignoring the interruptions, spoke softly, her voice barely audible to anyone but Alicia. "Alicia, your memories won't upset you. You'll see them like a film on a television screen. You won't be afraid. How old were you?"

"I think…three…maybe four. I don't remember. But I do remember every night when I went to bed, a big black cat would come in and curl up beside me. I used to cuddle it. I told my mother but she laughed and said I must have been dreaming. Then one night, she came in to say goodnight. I can still see the look of horror on her face. It wasn't a cat. It was a big black rat. She screamed…and it bit me."

She placed a finger on her cheek where a faint scar was just visible. James groaned. "Stop Alicia darling. Please stop."

But Alicia seemingly was oblivious now to anything and anyone but Pippa.

"A couple or so years after that when I was about six, there was an explosion at the pit where my dad worked and he was killed. My mother found work. Cleaning in a big house. As big as a castle I thought."

"Was it this one, Alicia? Was it Bishop Grange?"

Alicia nodded. "She said she used to work there years ago. In service she said. When she was a young girl. She had to take me to work with her during the school holidays. The first day she woke me early. It was really cold but she wrapped me up with a big scarf and we ran to catch a bus. We walked a long way when we got off the bus. Through big iron gates and up a really long path to the house. I remember there were trees on both sides. She walked very fast and she was dragging me along but I didn't cry because I knew she wanted to be on time."

Alicia paused. "I...can't remember anymore."

Pippa stroked the back of her hand. "Yes you can," she coaxed. "Take your time."

The door opened and Inspector Locky slipped quietly into the room and sat down next to James. Pippa turned to him, motioning him to be quiet.

Alicia began to speak again. "I remember two big lions outside the front door. The door had studs on it. But we couldn't go in the front door. We had to walk round to the back. A big fat woman with a red face opened the door. She had the reddest face I'd ever seen. Yes...I remember. She was the Cook. Not the one here now though. My mother was only little and she had to do all the scrubbing. In the hall, there were stone flags and she scrubbed them every day. Her hands were always rough and smelled of soap. I had to stay in the kitchen and sometimes she'd come in and give me cuddle but I hated that. Her apron was coarse and damp. I did love her though. I didn't like to see her working so hard. She was always so tired when we came home. But we needed the money."

"Do you want to rest, Alicia?" asked Pippa.

Alicia ignored her and spoke quickly, as if worried she may forget.

"The lady of the house frightened me. When she came near my heart would bump. She couldn't walk. She was in a wheelchair, always dressed in black and her eyes looked black, like big buttons. She used to wrinkle her nose whenever she saw me as if there was a nasty smell. I knew she didn't like me. Didn't like me being there. I didn't like her either. I think I hated her even though my mother used to say you shouldn't hate anybody. One day I wandered into the dining room where a maid was laying the table for dinner that night. The Master...Mr George I think he was called...he wasn't there every day...he patted me on the head and the lady saw him. She shouted at him and said 'don't do that. That's the daily's child. She might have nits'. I remember feeling so ashamed. I thought only dirty children had nits and I wanted to tell him I was a clean little girl. But before I could open my mouth

120

I was yanked away by the maid and sat roughly on a chair in the kitchen. 'You stay there', she said 'and don't go roaming where you shouldn't. Your Mam'll get the sack if you don't behave. I'll bet she'll be glad when you go back to school'.

I had a whole summer at the house. There were two daughters, Maud and Grace. Grace was at boarding school and Maud was at a college. When they came home for the holidays, the lady made me call them Miss Maud and Miss Grace. I didn't like having to call them Miss just because my Mam was their cleaning woman."

James eyes filled with tears as he listened. He was beginning to understand his wife. She'd been proud even as a child. He knew now why she always had to have the best.

"I remember seeing Leo. He didn't notice me, of course." Alicia paused for a few seconds and then continued. "The sisters let me play in the garden. They showed me their hideaway. A tree-house. It wasn't high in the trees, just built round the trunk of a tree. I loved it. The sides were so high they seemed to stretch right up to the sky."

James gasped as he heard her words, recalling her account of her dream. 'The walls extend up into the sky,' she had said. 'Like skyscrapers disappearing into cloud'.

James turned to Harry and whispered. "I don't like this. I must stop it Harry."

But Harry remained silent and Alicia carried on speaking.

"One day I fell asleep in it. When they found me, my Mam was white and shaking. She'd thought I was lost. The girls were laughing at her and the lady said I was a pest and she'd be glad to see the back of me."

Icy fingers gripped James' heart as his wife continued with relentless determination. With growing apprehension and increasing horror, he recalled Miss Maud's account of her mother's death. He wanted to shout to her. Tell her to stop. That she was about to destroy herself, but the words would not come out.

"One day I got bored in the kitchen and wandered out again, this time into the hall. Before me was a long staircase. I walked up it, gazing at the pictures on the wall. Beautiful women, handsome men. I felt happy, just looking at them. I wasn't doing any harm. At the top of the stairs there was a long corridor with doors on either side and one at the end of the corridor facing me. I walked towards it and I heard the handle being turned. In a panic

I turned to run back down the stairs. But she shouted for me to stop. It was the lady. She wheeled herself along the corridor shouting at me for being there, telling me that I belonged in the kitchen. When we were both at the top of the stairs she told me to go down and fetch that woman to help her down the stairs.

She meant my Mam. I wanted to cry. Tell her that my Mam was too tired. But I just shook my head. She grabbed my arm and squeezed it hard. I remember yelling in pain and she smiled, her big black button eyes staring into mine. She was enjoying hurting me. I pushed the chair and it toppled over. It went faster and faster, swaying from side to side like a drunk. Then it rolled over at the bottom."

James closed his eyes in despair. What was it Miss Maud had said? 'My mother was murdered. It was the cleaning lady's child. A sweet little girl'. Oh Alicia my love. Stop. Please stop.

Harry was becoming concerned about Fran. The two women seemed to have been under Pippa's influence for an inordinate length of time. He coughed, trying to catch Pippa's attention and she half turned towards him, still keeping careful watch over her subjects. He pointed questioningly to Fran who was snoring away happily in the corner of the settee. Pippa smiled briefly, and nodded, indicating that Fran was perfectly safe in her hands. Alicia began to speak again, reverting back now to her native Yorkshire dialect.

"Mi Mam were standin' in the 'all. I ran to 'er an' buried mi 'ead in 'er apron."

She became noticeably agitated and Pippa sat down beside her and held both her hands. "You're doing fine, Alicia," she said soothingly. "Take your time now."

"She squeezed me tight. So tight I could hardly breath. There was a buzzing in my ears like strange music. After that I must have fainted. Someone had put an icepack on my head and the Cook was standing over me. I could hear a whimpering sound. I looked around expecting to see a frightened puppy or a kitten. But there was nothing. And I realized the sound was coming from me."

There followed a long and ominous silence. Pippa stood up.

"Alicia, I want you to remember everything you've told me when you awake. I want you to wake up...*now*."

Alicia opened her eyes, looking slightly bemused. And then she remembered. "I saw the tree house today when I was walking in the garden. It looked so familiar but I didn't know why. Not until now. It looked so small today."

No one spoke. Each had their own thoughts on what was going to happen next. Inspector Locky had been joined by Sergeant McTavish, both sitting in quiet contemplation.

James stood up and held out his arms to his wife. She moved towards him and he gathered her to him. His chest was tightening and the blood pounded in his head. He knew what she was going to say next.

"I'm sorry James. I'm so sorry."

She began to cry and he sat her down on the settee.

"Alicia," he began desperately. "Please darling, don't say any more."

But Alicia ignored him. "When we arrived here I had this incredible feeling of déjà vu. As soon as the house came into view. The trees, the lions, everything about the place. I felt I'd seen it all before. And when I saw Miss Maud I felt I knew her. But it was her mother I was seeing. Sarah Hepplewhite."

Her face crumpled. "It was me. I killed Miss Maud, James. I thought it was a dream but now I know it wasn't. She asked me to take her upstairs, remember. As I helped her into bed she touched my face. She touched my scar with her fingers. And she said 'Goodnight…sweet Alice.' That's my name. Not Alicia. I…didn't know what she meant. Only that she knew something dreadful about me and that I knew she musn't tell anyone. I left her and went to bed. I went straight to sleep. I must have woken and you weren't there, James."

"Oh God," James agonized silently. "I was downstairs. Drunk. I wasn't there for you, Alicia."

"I got out of bed. I knew where I had to go. I walked along the corridor and into Miss Maud's room. Those strange white shapes came swooping down on me again and the whimpering noises that I'd thought were strange music. Something heavy pressed down on me but this time I wasn't frightened. This time I didn't leave the room. I knew what I must do. I knew I musn't let Miss Maud tell anyone. Tell that I was Alice. Sweet Alice. I took the cushion out of her wheelchair and placed it on her face. I kept it there for a long time. When I took it off I didn't look at her. I didn't hurt her, James. I wouldn't…couldn't hurt her. She just went to sleep. I couldn't bear it if I'd hurt her. I'd hurt her mother, you see. When I pushed her down the stairs.

But I wanted to hurt *her*. I wanted her to be dead. I must have been *wicked* Alice. Not sweet Alice. I placed the cushion back in the chair and went to the bathroom. I was sick. I felt so ill. When I woke the next morning I was sure I'd been dreaming again. But…I hadn't, had I?"

Inspector Locky glanced at his sergeant and nodded.

"I think, Mr Brent," said Sergeant McTavish gently, "your wife will have to come to the station with me."

Chapter Twenty

Harry handed Pippa a large brandy. "Well done my dear," he said quietly. Pippa smiled at him, her big blue eyes bright with unshed tears.

"Thanks Harry. I'm knackered. I really am. I didn't tell you but it's the first time I've done it by myself. I always had Marvo watching over me. I do know what I'm doing though," she added hastily. "It's too dangerous to mess about with." Her tears spilled over and ran unchecked down her face. "Poor Alicia. Poor James."

"Don't cry Pippa. You had to do it." Harry handed her a tissue. He desperately wanted to wipe her tears away himself but thought it would be imprudent of him. Fran probably wouldn't understand.

But Fran was still in a hypnotic trance and still snoring quietly.

"Pippa, do you think it's time to...er...bring Fran back to us?" Harry was shocked to find himself thinking he would be perfectly happy to leave her as she was.

"Oops." Pippa giggled nervously. "Silly me. She's alright though. She'll have had a good rest. And she will be aware of what's been going on. Fran, when you awake your backache will have gone. Wake up Fran."

"I must say Pippa, I found that fascinating," said Tom. "I've often toyed with the idea of taking a course in hypnosis myself. A few of my colleagues use it and find it a tremendous help. How on earth did you become so expert? And how did you know that Alicia would be such a good subject?"

Tom questioned her enthusiastically. Her performance had fired his imagination. It was food for thought for when he moved to Australia. He glanced at Maggie. He hadn't told her yet of his decision. He knew it was going to be a difficult time for both of them. But they'd had their warning and he knew it was their only hope of ever leading a normal life.

"I don't really know Tom." Pippa shook her head. "Experience, I suppose. I used to help Marvo, my stage partner a lot." Pippa felt that now she'd performed solo she was entitled to elevate her position from assistant to a more prestigious position. "He relied on me to select the most likely subjects. I was never wrong. I knew she would be easy. And remember, she was completely relaxed because she wasn't expecting to be hypnotised. And so she just...went. I couldn't have done it without Fran though."

"Ah," said Tom. "So...you and Fran had arranged it?"

"Oh yes. And Inspector Locky."

"So come on Pippa. Tell us how you knew it was Alicia?" asked Maggie, curiously.

"I didn't. I thought it *could* be. What I was sure of was that it couldn't have been Aggie. And...well, Leo's a pain in the arse sometimes but he's not killer. The inspector'll be bringing him and Aggie back. I'd better not say anymore until they arrive."

Lucy popped her head round the door. "Now then you lot. 'ow many fer dinner?"

Harry looked around the room. "Just the five of us, Lucy."

Lucy's eyes opened wide as she followed his gaze around the room. "Where is everybody?"

Harry shook his head despairingly. "Don't ask girl. Don't ask."

Lucy returned to the kitchen. "Yer know Mam, it's like playing ten green bleedin' bottles in this 'ouse. Folk's is disappearing afore mi very eyes."

"Stop talkin' rubbish an' get these 'ere tureens on t'table."

"I say Mam...what do yer think Mr Leo'll think about 'avin' a skivvy forra Mam. 'An not just an ordinary skivvy. A murderin' skivvy. I wish it 'ad been 'im that 'ad done in Miss Maud an' not poor old Aggie. Alright. I'm off."

Cook, exasperated by her daughter's incessant chatter threw a tea towel at her.

Within seconds Lucy had bounced back excitedly into the kitchen. "Mr Leo's back. And Aggie. It weren't 'er, Mam. Mam *listen* will yer? Guess who it were. That stuck up Mrs Brent. 'Er and Mr Brent have bin taken in."

"That'll be six now fer dinner then." Cook was beyond being surprised.

"Can't yer count, Mam? Seven. I said Mr. Leo and Aggie."

"Aggie dun't count," said her mother flatly.

....

A subdued and thoughtful Leo took his place at the head of the table, leaving Inspector Locky and Aggie standing. Harry coughed dryly, noisily pushed back his chair and rose from the table. Bravely risking Leo's wrath, he invited the inspector to join them. Pippa glanced covertly at her lover, waiting for him to rebuke Harry for usurping his position. But Leo merely nodded to the inspector and motioned to Aggie to take a seat.

"You'll both be hungry. Best get something to eat."

The inspector hesitated, aware that he had pressing duties awaiting him at the station but the sight and smell of Lily's culinary skills overcame his natural sense of duty. Most of his meals were taken in the police canteen and he momentarily allowed himself to lapse into a state of self hypnosis, visualizing Lily bustling around *his* kitchen, producing steaming steak and kidney puddings and appetising apple pies.

"Thank you. I will. I do have some points to clear up here. And tomorrow, I'm sure you'll all be pleased to know you'll be able to go home. Aggie?" he inquired, pulling a chair out for her.

Aggie shook her head. "Not mi place, sir. I'll go an' see if Cook wants an' 'and."

All eyes were on Leo.

"Let her be," he said quietly.

"Mr Hepplewhite." The Inspector sat down next to him. "I don't know if you realize yet what a debt of gratitude we owe to your...friend Pippa. Her intuition and observations may have avoided a grave miscarriage of justice."

"Oh aye. Well...it was 'er that got me arrested. Blabbin' on about me goin' out to t'bathroom during t'night."

Pippa smiled to herself as she recognized Leo's slight return to his Yorkshire dialect after only a short time back here. And she was delighted that her ability to detect accents had not deserted her. But her voice was grave as she spoke.

"You were away a long time Leo. I *had* to tell the inspector. You couldn't have just been in the bathroom. I stayed awake for ages. In the end I fell asleep."

Leo looked flustered. "Actually Pip, you're right. I told the inspector. I went to look in cousin Maud's desk. To see if I could find a copy of her will."

"And...did you find what you were looking for?" smiled Harry facetiously, knowing that all copies of Maud's will were safely tucked away in his firm's safe.

Maggie interrupted impatiently. "Inspector, can't you tell us now what happened. At least, can Pippa tell us why she suspected Alicia. I think we're entitled to know."

"No Miss," replied Locky mildly. "You're not entitled to anything. However, under the circumstances, if Pippa feels she wants to tell you then of course I can't stop her."

Pippa looked around her shyly. Used as she was to performing in front of large crowds without any inhibitions, to find herself the centre of attention within a small group was a new experience.

"Well...the evening we arrived here, Alicia insisted that this was her first visit to Yorkshire. I knew it couldn't be. She has a very slight Yorkshire accent. Not much, but it's there if you listen carefully. I'm a bit of an expert I suppose on regional accents. Because of my stage training, you see."

Her tone was almost apologetic, as if she had no right to be knowledgeable on any subject and Harry, touched by her humility, felt a sudden urge of protectiveness towards her.

"And then there was the ring. Her solitaire ring. It was stuck in the cushion. At the time I assumed it had happened when she plumped up the cushion...remember...before she helped her upstairs. And I don't know if anyone noticed, but Aggie called her Alice. Miss Alice, she said. I think Aggie knew who she was, as well as Miss Maud. I spoke to Cook. She wasn't here at the time, of course, but she had heard Aggie talk about the cleaning lady's little girl and she remembered her name. Alice. Sweet Alice, everyone used to call her. Alicia had spoken to me about her dream. I felt it could be connected with her childhood. You know what they say about a dream being a repressed and forbidden wish. Well, I'm sure Alicia was punishing herself for what she'd done by repeatedly reliving the horror. Blaming herself for Sarah Hepplewhite's death even though she couldn't remember anything about it. She'd pushed it to the back of her mind. The hypnosis helped her to age-regress...to go back in time...and as soon as she remembered she realized what she'd done. I knew she *wanted* to understand why the dream kept recurring so I knew that, once under hypnosis, she would co-operate. People won't do anything against their will, you see. But the most important thing was..." Pippa paused and shuddered as she recalled her revulsion, "when I went into Miss Maud's bedroom...you know...when I heard Lucy screaming...I touched Miss Maud's face. It was cold."

Pippa covered her face with her hands. There was a sympathetic silence as the girl struggled to recover her composure. Taking a deep breath, she continued. "Aggie couldn't have killed her, could she? If she had...Miss Maud would still have been warm."

She began to cry bitterly. "I'd...never seen a dead person before. It was horrible."

"So was Aggie only protecting you, Leo?" asked Tom. "Did she believe that you'd killed your cousin?"

Leo, tracing imaginary patterns with a fork on the crisp white linen, made no reply.

"No, she didn't." Inspector Locky, now mellowed with the continuing flow of wine from the Hepplewhite cellar, was prepared to talk. "In fact, in her mind she knew Leo was innocent."

He hesitated before saying more, unsure whether he should continue or not. He glanced at Leo. But Leo did not raise his eyes from his preoccupation and so he continued.

"Aggie did go into Maud's room intending to kill her. She said that when she put the cushion over Maud's face, Maud didn't move. What Aggie didn't know was, the reason she didn't move was because she was already dead. And had been dead for several hours. But...it was Aggie who left the cushion on Maud's face. And of course, Lucy found her a few minutes later.

Leo, with a sudden movement threw the fork away from him.

"I shall sue you of course, Inspector. For wrongful arrest." However, his threat was made without conviction and no one, including Inspector Locky, believed him.

"I'm off to bed," said Leo brusquely, realizing that the inspector was not going to rise to the bait. "Come on Pippa."

Pippa shook her head and Leo left the room.

....

"Now you listen ter me Aggie. You sit yer sen down in my chair by t'stove an' Lucy'll get yer summet to eat. I'll finish this washin' up mi sen. You've bin through a terrible time."

"Ee Lily. I can't eat a thing. Just...let me sit 'ere forra bit."

Cook pulled up another chair and sat opposite the tired old woman.

"What we gonna do, Aggie?" she asked wearily. "Do yer think Mr Leo'll keep this 'ouse goin'? An' what'll 'appen to my lass?"

"Mam, I've telt yer. I want ter go back to school."

"Aye well...them that wants niver gets. How *can* yer, lass? Yer need to gerra job somewhere. Yer can't waste yer time at school. What yer want ter do that for anyway?"

"I want ter be a solicitor," answered Lucy eagerly.

"Don't you be gerrin' any daft ideas. Don't you be gerrin' out of yer own class," said her mother fearfully.

"Bless the boss and all his race and help to keep us in our place," quoted Lucy, sarcastically pulling her fringe. "It's you that's daft Mam. Yer livin' in t'past. Mrs Gough said I could if I worked 'ard. An' I'll 'ave elocution lessons. Learn ter speak nice."

"Stop that," said her mother indignantly. "There's nowt wrong wi a good Yorkshire accent an'don't you forget it. Don't ever be ashamed of where yer cum' from."

"I won't Mam. An' I'll never be ashamed of mi roots. It's just that...oh you tell 'er Aggie. You can speak nice when yer want. I 'eard yer."

"She's right Lily. Let the lass gerraway if she can. There's got ter be more to life than scrubbing."

"See," said Lucy triumphantly. "I'll do it. I promise. I'm clever enough. Mam, I'm really tired. Can I go ter bed?"

"Not till yer've finished 'ere yer can't."

"Let the lass go Lily," said Aggie softly. "I'll 'elp ter finish off."

Lucy stared in surprise at her unexpected ally. After a moment's hesitation, she walked over to her and kissed her wrinkled face. "Thanks Aggie. I'm reight glad yer back."

Aggie took hold of her arm, gripping it tightly. "Promise me you'll do it Lucy. Promise," she said urgently.

Lucy nodded. "I will Aggie. I promise."

She turned to her mother, desperate for some sign of encouragement from her, but none came.

"Goodnight then, Mam."

Her mother, arms deep in washing up water chose not to hear her, working on the principle that if she ignored her daughter's aspirations they would go away. Not that she was uncaring. On the contrary. She was afraid of Lucy being hurt. Of having her hopes dashed. And with typical Yorkshire possessiveness...she was frightened of losing her.

....

"Right Aggie. All dun. Let's get ter bed."

Cook gave the draining board a final wipe, cast a proud eye around her spotless kitchen and with a sigh, removed her apron and hung it on a hook behind the door.

"Aggie," she began, hesitantly. "Yer've been a brick all these years. I mean…about Mr Leo. It must 'ave been 'ard for yer. Did yer never want ter tell 'im?"

Aggie sat down again in the old rocking chair. "Nay las. 'Ow could I? I'd 'ave been that ashamed."

"Has he said anything to yer?"

"He owes me nowt," said Aggie simply.

Cook shook her head, reflecting that she, at least, had been able to keep her girl.

"Aggie, do yer think yer should encourage t'lass ter think them daft things? I mean, going back ter school an' that?"

The old woman gazed at her sadly. "Lucy's right Lily. We're livin' in t'past. This might be *our* station. But it's not 'ers. She's right ter want somethin' better than us."

"It'll cost," said Cook desperately. "I've no money, Aggie. 'Ow can she go back ter school? We might not even 'ave anywhere ter live soon."

"Get yersen to bed, Lily. Yer tired."

"Aye. I am. Are you comin' then?"

Aggie stretched out her dry wrinkled hands to the heat. "In a minute. You go. I'll see yer tomorrer. It's…a bit cold in my room."

"Well, don't stay up too long. Yer've 'ad an 'ard day."

Aggie closed her eyes and Cook, although reluctant to leave, departed from her kitchen, closing the door quietly behind her.

Chapter Twenty-One

As the early dawn crept over the mellow stone of Bishop Grange, the once imposing and gracious old building awaited its fate in dignified silence as the finger of fate tightened its grip. The snow had melted from the rooftop and the signs of dilapidation and deterioration revealed themselves once more, starkly accusing generations of Hepplewhites, all of whom had failed it. Failed a house that had stoutly sheltered them through prosperity and poverty. Bishop Grange was about to acquire a new owner. An owner who would do no more for it than had his predecessors. An owner who had no more regard for the proud old building than he would have had for an old jacket worn threadbare by constant use.

A playful breeze flirted with the broken window shutters causing them to protest piteously, the weakness of their creaking barely registering with the slumbering occupants. Except one. Young Lucy had been awake most of the night, hugging herself in gleeful anticipation of what life may yet hold for her. Her youthful enthusiasm and optimism took no account of the economics of her ambitions. She looked to the future and what she saw now was not a life of drudgery, but the glittering prize of wealth and importance, with a position in a society which her mother and Aggie had been content to serve.

In spite of the bitter cold Lucy jumped out of bed willingly, splashed her face quickly in icy cold water, pulled on her clothes and ran down the stairs to start her chores. As the clock struck six, two fires responding obediently to Lucy's enthusiasm were burning brightly. The dining room table was laid ready for what Lucy hoped would be the last breakfast, and that all the remaining guests would be leaving this morning for their respective homes.

Happily and tunefully singing 'Nymphs and Shepherds', Lucy skipped into the kitchen to stoke up the Aga. She switched on the light and stamped her feet, keeping her eyes tightly closed to give any mouse that may have ventured in time to scurry back to its hole. But as the flickering light gave way to brilliance, her singing trailed off to a breathless gasp as she stared at the motionless figure sitting in her mother's rocking chair. She approached the chair nervously, never taking her eyes off the black-clad form.

"Aggie. What yer gorrup so early for?"

But Lucy knew instinctively her newly found ally had not risen at the crack of dawn.

"Oooh, *no*."

She dropped to her knees in front of the chair. She felt no fear as she stretched out a trembling hand to touch the silent figure.

"Aggie. Oh Aggie, don't go."

But Aggie was dead. Lucy fell back on her heels, wondering why she was not afraid, as she had been when she'd found Miss Maud. She gazed at the tiny face, never pretty even in childhood. But in death Aggie's features had acquired a serenity that she'd never found during her long, arduous years. And Lucy cried for her. She cried for Aggie's lost youth. For the degradation of the rape carried out so cruelly by George Hepplewhite. For the sorrow of having her child taken from her. For the dignity with which she had carried out her duties. And Lucy solemnly promised Aggie once again that she would strive to achieve her goal.

"What thi 'ell…?"

Lucy lifted a tear-stained face up to her mother.

"I think she'd 'ad enough, Mam."

………………….

"Well…the doctor seems positive there's no question of any foul play here. I think Lucy's right. I think poor Aggie just gave up."

Inspector Locky glanced at Leo, hoping to see some sign of grieving in his expression, but Leo's face remained impassive.

"Have you given any thought Mr Hepplewhite, as to what will happen to Cook and her girl?"

But if Inspector Locky was hoping to infuse a little social conscience into Leo, he might have found it easier to persuade a cuckoo to build its own nest.

Leo shrugged his shoulders. "Not really my concern is it? Maud should have seen to that."

Harry Gough coughed, took off his spectacles and began to polish them. "I know that at this stage I'm probably speaking prematurely but I do feel, in the uncertain circumstances of Cook and Lucy, it would be judicious of me to reveal some of the contents of Miss Maud's will." He replaced his spectacles carefully. "And also of Aggie's, even though the poor lady is only just deceased. I wonder please, if someone would ask Cook to come in to the sitting room. And Lucy of course."

Maggie and Tom McCriel exchanged glances. "Do you think Inspector, that we could be making tracks? We do have a long journey and none of this is our concern."

Inspector Locky frowned. "If you could hang on a little longer. I would like a word with Mr McCriel before you go. Ah…here's the coffee. Thanks Lucy. No…don't go. Your mother's coming in too. Mr Gough wants to speak to you."

"Yes, do please all sit down. This won't take long. Is everyone here now?"

"All except Pippa." Fran started to struggle to her feet. "I'll fetch her."

"No. No, don't bother," said Harry quickly. "You Leo, as you are aware, are Miss Maud's heir. The whole of the estate is bequeathed to you. There are however, some monies left to Cook which should facilitate her until she finds another post, assuming that you intend to dispose of Bishop Grange. And…Miss Maud left Aggie £100,0000."

"That'll be mine now," said Leo quickly.

Harry viewed Leo over the top of his spectacles, relishing the news he was about to impart.

"No Leo. It will not be yours. Aggie was aware of Miss Maud's will and in her own will has left it all to Lucy."

Leo's mouth opened and shut without a sound escaping from it.

"Shut it, Leo. You look like a fish."

Pippa entered the room dressed in a long pale blue cape, trimmed with a darker blue velvet collar. And provocatively perched on her head, a matching blue velvet hat from under which her blonde curls cascaded luxuriantly. She lowered her suitcase to the floor and smiled brightly.

"Well…I suppose its time we went."

"Yes Harry," sighed Fran. "We'd better pack our cases too. We've been away long enough. You're wearing the last of your clean underpants."

"My case is packed, Fran."

"I'll go and do mine then."

Fran swung her legs backwards and forwards to assist her ascent from the depths of the chair.

Harry took off his spectacles, folded them and placed them in his pocket.

"I won't be coming home, Fran. I'm giving up the practice. I never wanted to be a solicitor, you know. I wanted to be a ventriloquist. I bought a dummy and I used to practice in front of a mirror. In the privacy of my bedroom of course. I was good. But I was expected to follow my father into the family firm, as he did after his father. One did not go against one's parents' wishes. Pippa's going to teach me the business. Show business, that is.

She knows all there is to know. Practically born in a suitcase weren't you, my love?"

Pippa nodded. That wasn't strictly true. Her parents had had a fish and chip shop in Rochdale but Pippa knew it didn't do to reveal too much of one's background in the world of entertainment.

"We're going to be partners. On the stage. Hypnotists. I'll be Pippa's assistant. You'll be alright, Fran. For money I mean. I'm sorry Fran," added Harry desperately. "It's my last chance. And Pippa loves me."

Inspector Locky shook his head despairingly. No fool like an old fool. Fran collapsed back into the deep chair, gasping and fanning herself with a magazine. Had James still been there he would have seen at first hand what was meant by the 'vapours'.

Leo roared like a frustrated bull. "You cow. You've been having it off with him all the time we've been here."

"Oh no Leo." Pippa shook her head. "I don't cheat. You should know that. But…well, Harry and me…we're right for one another. We *gel*. And I *will* teach him all I know. And he's going to teach me. About words and things. And anyway Leo, I don't really like you very much. You're a prurient old sod."

Harry smiled at her proudly as they left the room together. She was going to be a fast learner.

…………………..

Maggie and Tom departed after Inspector Locky had extracted again from Tom the promise he'd made to emigrate to Australia. Without Maggie.

Leo left the house in a rage, swearing profusely and threatening to contest Aggie's will. Fran, weeping copiously had waddled into a taxi after raiding the fridge, saying she would *die* if she didn't have something to eat.

Lucy, for once speechless, was wandering around the house in a daze. Inspector Locky found Cook in the kitchen scrubbing her old pine table.

"Stop that for a minute, will you Lily?"

"Ee Thomas. Am that glad yer 'ere. I need ter talk ter somebody."

"I want to talk to you too. Lily, what's your plans? Do you have anywhere to go?"

She shook her head. "Its bin too quick. 'Aven't 'ad chance ter think."

"Leo'll not keep this place on, you know. As I understand, he's going ahead

135

with this low-cost housing scheme. This old place'll be demolished. Why don't you come and work for me? Keep house. I'm on my own and it's a big house I've got. No strings attached Lily," he added quickly as doubt clouded her eyes. "I'll be retiring soon. Could do with a bit o' company and...some good grub. Think about it, will you? And a home for Lucy. Be good to have a young 'un around for a bit."

"Thomas, it's 'er I want ter talk about. I'm at mi wits end. She wants to tek up soliciting."

Thomas stared at her aghast. "My god, Lily. What's the girl thinking about? You must stop her."

"I know. I telt 'er. It's daft 'er goin'back ter school at 'er age."

He looked puzzled. "Back to school?"

"I don't know where she gets 'er ideas from. An' Aggie were no better. Telling 'er she should better 'ersen."

Thomas smiled as it slowly dawned on him what she meant. "I see. Well, in that case you'd better accept my offer, Lily. Then we can both keep an eye on her. I think, with a mother like you, she'll make a very good solicitor. I'm sure you'll keep her feet firmly on the ground."

....

Lucy sat on the kitchen table swinging her legs. "Did 'ee really say that, Mam? An' are yer goin' ter shack up wi Thomas?"

"You show some respect, Lucy. Inspector Locky to you. And no. I'm not shackin' up wi' 'im. I'm gonna do for him." But her mother blushed as she remembered Thomas' searching, demanding kisses all those years ago. And she remembered too, her passionate response. "Anyway, I think we should lass. Nowt 'ere for us is there? An' you'll be able ter go back ter school if that's what yer really want."

"It is Mam. 'Ave never bin so sure of anything as this. Will I 'ave mi own bedroom?"

"Aye, yer will."

"I can't believe it. It's like a dream. Yer know Mam, it's right what that Maggie Thatcher said."

"What d'yer mean, Lucy?"

"Well, when yer think about it, a few days ago I were a skivvy. Today I'm an' 'eiress an' I'm going ter be a solicitor. And...mi own bedroom. I'll be able ter read all night if I want."

"What's that got ter do wi' that Maggie Thatcher."

"Well, didn't she say 'It's a funny old world'?"

Her mother laughed and in a rare display of affection hugged her close.

"Gerrof. But seriously Mam. Thanks fer 'avin' me. An' thank that butcher an'all…if yer can find 'im."

Lucy leaped from the table laughing gleefully and ran out of the kitchen, followed by a wet dishcloth.

END